Judith E. Spörl

Lena Earns Her Wings

Translated by Brendan English
Cover and illustrations by Doreen Goedhart

www.tredition.de

© 2018 Judith E. Spörl

Published & printed by tredition GmbH, Halenreie 40-44, 22359 Hamburg, Germany
Cover and illustrations by Doreen Goedhart
Translation by Brendan English
Proof Reading by James Cowling, David English, Joanna Rain Vincent, Abbey Martin, Marie English, Ailsa McMillan

ISBN
Paperback: 978-3-7439-4676-7
Hardcover: 978-3-7439-4677-4
e-Book: 978-3-7439-4678-1

For Merle

1. At School

It was much too warm and stuffy in the classroom. Lena and her classmates had been breathing stale, stagnant air and concentrating, more or less, on their English for over an hour. Outside, a typical German April snow flurry was sweeping over the schoolyard. Mrs Ott, their year 8 English teacher, didn't want any windows opened in this weather. While the students sweated over their test, she sat there, frozen as ever, and sipped at a cup of milky tea. It was a strange old habit of hers. She never came to class without a large thermos of tea.

Naturally everyone had suspected that there might be more than just tea in the thermos at first, until one time, one of the boys had dared to have a taste when Mrs Ott was out for a while. Disappointingly it hadn't turned out to be an alcoholic delicacy. It really was just tea with milk as was only proper for a true Briton.

'Only another ten minutes kids, time is ticking!' trilled Mrs Ott. Lena sighed. Isabella, who was sitting next to her, stretched her back briefly, pulled her blond ponytail up a bit tighter and bent over her work again.

I wonder what Kim is doing right now? Lena's thoughts drifted off. I wonder if she already has new friends? In an email Kim had vaguely said the new school was OK. Kim's family had moved from Holzhausen to Berlin two months ago. Her father had been transferred at work. Kim planned to visit Lena in the spring and summer school holidays and in the meantime they kept each other busy with emails. Lena kept Kim up to date with every detail from school, especially about Philipp. Kim had a *huuuge* crush on Philipp. Lena glanced briefly behind her. At that moment Philipp was staring at the back of Isabella's head with a vacant expression on his face. When he noticed that Lena had caught him at it, he grimaced and kept writing. So he *was* after Isabella after all. She should have known. Lena started composing her next mail to Kim in her imagination.

Once, they had all been a cool clique. Kim, Lena, Philipp (who lived three doors down), Philipp's buddy Martin and Isabella with her shadow and best friend Katy. Somehow that had all melted away. Philipp was always somewhere or other with his football team, presumably dragging Martin along with him. Isabella and Katy were just, simply, annoying. They acted like overly chic smart alecs all of a sudden. They were somehow totally "in". That wasn't Lena's world. Now Kim had moved away too! Philipp wasn't much better than Isabella, so very cool and full of himself. Isabella and Katy lapped it up, at least they were always giggling whenever he was nearby. Martin didn't seem to mind as much as Lena did though.

'Have you finished, dear?' asked Mrs Ott.

Lena had been daydreaming and hadn't written anything for several minutes. She blushed.

'Sorry Mrs Ott.' Lena mumbled her apology and quickly scribbled the last few sentences before the bell rang. Mrs Ott always used English in class and expected the pupils to do so too.

'Everybody put down your pens now!' called Mrs Ott over the rising din. The first few students were already handing in their papers and charging out the door. Others were still trying to squeeze out one or two extra points in the last few seconds. Lena laid her work on the stack on the teacher's desk and followed Isabella and the others outside. Isabella immediately started chewing over the whole test with Katy.

'What did you put for number 9...yeah I don't know, it was like *so* easy, did I miss something or what?'

Lena rolled her eyes and hurried to overtake them. She hated these post mortems. It was done now and that was good. She didn't want to let herself be driven crazy by hearing any more about it. One music class to go and it would be the weekend.

After Music, Lena was first onto the school bus to Holzhausen and hid herself in the corner of the last seat. She pulled a thick book out of her bag and buried herself in the story. Without Kim, her favourite pastime had become reading. Lena's mother worked in a bookshop, so she had no shortage of books. The bus would have to take a long circuitous route to Holzhausen. There were a lot of stops to make on the way, so Lena had almost half an hour's reading time. Isabella held court up the front of the bus and was the centre of attention as usual. Lena realized, not quite without envy, that Katy, Philipp, a couple of his football mates, Martin, everyone and everything naturally revolved around Isabella.

She buried her nose deeper in her book.

Lena, actually her full name was Lena Maria Reisenberg, lived with her mother Barbara, Barbara's partner Johannes, and Lena's seven-year-old half brother Jakob. Her parents had split up when she was still quite small. However, she had a very good relationship with her father, Paul Reisenberg. Fortunately, her parents had managed to part on good terms. When Jakob had arrived on the scene, the patchwork family had moved into a semi-detached house in Holzhausen. Johannes didn't have too far to go from there to the hospital where he worked as a ward physician.

Paul Reisenberg lived some distance away from Holzhausen. He was a pilot with a private company and always travelled a lot. Paul came to Holzhausen two or three times a month and he and Lena always did something together: cinema, swimming or just ambling around and talking. Sometimes on the weekends, Lena went to his place in Kirchheim. She got on well with his partner Regina and the three of them went walking or cycling together. A few times they had even taken Jakob along. He found it so unfair that his big sister always got to go on these special outings without him.

Lena was glad when the bus finally arrived. She let the others get ahead of her and slowly dawdled home. Grandma Liesl, Barbara's mother, was bustling around in the kitchen frying potato pancakes. Lena gave her a kiss on the cheek on the way past.

'Hello Grandma!'

Jakob was already sitting at the kitchen table munching appreciatively with his mouth full.

'Hello Sweetie,' Grandma Liesl greeted her cheerfully. 'Come here and sit down! Your mother's coming later. How was school? Your father called, he says he'll pick you up on Sunday morning and – Jakob get your fingers out of the apple sauce, the spoon is THERE and…'

'I want to go too,' interrupted Jakob, unmoved, with a whine, and continued to make a mess of the applesauce.

'Don't be silly, you don't even know what they're going to do dear, just you wait and see – and Lena your mother says you should please make sure you get out the books, she says you know which ones, for the flea market on Saturday, and you got an email from Kim, she wants to call you tonight – Jakob please!'

'But I want to go Grandma.'

'Work it out with Paul, you'll see him on Sunday morning anyway. Now come on Lena, sweetie, you haven't told us about your day yet. Do you want sugar?'

Lena sighed and started eating. She let Jakob and Grandma talk on. She couldn't get a word in edgeways anyhow. Straight after the meal, she briefly talked about her day at school and then ran up to her room.

2. Missing Kim

'Where's the box with the fantasy stories, Lena?' asked Barbara on Saturday morning. They had already put loads of cartons in the bookshop delivery van. Johannes was just bringing the next box up from the basement.

'It's already here, Mama.' All year they collected second hand books donated by friends and family for the spring flea market. The bookshop, where Lena's mother worked, held the flea market and the proceeds were given to charity.

Lena liked flea markets and enjoyed coming along and helping her mother every year. What she liked best though was fossicking around in the crates of old stories for herself. She always came home with a huge stack of new books.

This year she was also supposed to keep a lookout for new titles for Kim, who had given her a long list. They had talked on the phone last night – and afterwards Kim had written everything out again in detail in an email.

On the phone she had been quite ecstatic. Philipp had actually emailed her as well, now Kim was totally over the moon and even more infatuated than ever.

Lena had listened to her endless rave. Kim had been diligently deaf to the fact that Philipp had been worshiping Isabella's ponytail in class. His arrogant behaviour didn't disturb her overly either. She analyzed every word of his mail and wanted Lena to tell her how she should answer. Lena found that quite uncomfortable.

'Just write something about your new school,' she advised cautiously.

She was glad to be able to distract Kim a little with the flea market. Had Kim been here they could have worked over the subject much more easily. She and Kim would have gone to the flea market together, Grandma would have brought them warm apple pies and a pot of tea, they would have first made themselves quite comfortable behind the display table and then been able to talk freely. Mornings were often not so busy. Over such a distance though, she was starting to find her best friend's enthusiasm somewhat trying.

Soon all the boxes were in the van and they headed off. It was cold again, but it had finally stopped snowing. Lena had pulled on a parka over her denim jacket as well as gloves and a woolly hat. She didn't like how she looked in that outfit at all. Generally she never wore a beanie. She didn't think it suited her.

'Like the Michelin Man,' she railed. Her mother remained adamant though:

'You'll be standing around outside the whole day, IF YOU PLEASE!' By her tone of voice, she clearly wouldn't tolerate further objection. Two single strands of Lena's brown curly hair, her large brown eyes, and her nose were still visible. The rest of her was completely bundled up.

The book table was quickly set up. Barbara was still moving the car. Lena pushed the unpacked boxes under the table and distributed the books. Apart from themselves, other helpers were busy setting up and the first curious customers were already out and about looking for the best bargains.

Johannes and Jakob were going to come along later. They were sure to be at home making the most of the opportunity to play on the computer. Lena's mother didn't think much of that. She often sent the boys outside and of course it was always just at the moment that they found the most exciting.

Barbara came back with two steaming mugs.

'I've brought hot cocoa. Here you go. Brr, it's fresh today.' They both held their noses over their mugs and inhaled the warm steam, 'Do you want to take a look around for yourself Lena? It's not so full yet!' Lena sipped her cocoa. It was good.

'OK, I'll go soon.'

A little later she meandered off with Kim's list. Only two stands along she found the first book for Kim and another two for herself. The atmosphere at the flea market was friendly. Most of the visitors already knew each other from previous years.

Out of the corner of her eye, Lena saw that her mother too was already chatting to the other sellers and the first customers were looking through her books.

'Hiii Lena!' Someone called to her all of a sudden, 'you here again too? Let's see that. What've you found already?'

Lena turned around to see Isabella standing there, complete with flicking ponytail, pink earmuffs and a bright red jacket.

Of course, Lena realized, she was here last year too.

At the sight of Isabella, Lena mentally cursed her thick beanie and shapeless parka.

'Our stand's over there,

we've already sold heaps; I won't have to stand around here much longer today. It's such a drag, but my mother insists on it,' sighed Isabella theatrically and glanced at the books in Lena's hands.

'No way! They can't be for you surely? I read them all two years ago. We've got one of those subscriptions you know.'

'Err,' answered Lena feebly 'I don't know, I think they're OK, and this is for Kim, I'm still looking around …'

'Oh yeah Kim,' interrupted Isabella, 'haven't heard from her for ages, how's she doing these days? But tell me, your mother works in the bookshop, you're virtually at the source. Oh, here comes Philipp. About time too, I'm freezing, we're going into town you know.'

Sure enough, Philipp was casually walking towards them with his hands buried deep in his pockets. He had his long dark hair tied back and his ears were bright red from the cold.

'Hi girls.' He kissed Isabella on the cheek and nodded to Lena.

'Can we go?' he asked Isabella.

'No, I'm sure my mother won't let me go yet, but you have to give us a hand to move the table further into the sun anyway, come on! Ciao Lena, see you later. Why don't you have a look on our stand? You're sure to find cooler books there.'

Lena shifted her gaze from Isabella to Philipp, dumbfounded. Isabella had taken Philipp's hand and was snuggling up beside him.

'Hey Philipp,' Lena had composed herself quickly and remembered her brief, 'Kim said to say hello. She was very glad to get your email.' Isabella frowned. Philipp blushed.

'Are you coming?' Isabella was already pulling him away and the two of them disappeared into the maze of book tables.

Lena snorted angrily. Who did that bimbo think she was

anyway? What you read might be important, but when you read it certainly wasn't. What was the smug, superior act all about? What about Philipp? Did he really think that was so great? Yeah, and what about Kim? Lena's mood was thoroughly ruined. She so wished she had been quicker on the comeback and retaliated better. What would Kim have to say about the whole story?

Lena looked around for a bit longer, but she gave Isabella's table a wide berth. Later she saw Philipp and Isabella leaving the flea market, headed for town arm in arm. She scuttled back to her own bookstall and slammed the new books into one of the empty cartons.

'Tell me dear, you've got a terrible scowl on your face, what's wrong?' wondered her mother.

'Mama, can I maybe go home early with Johannes and Jakob, the whole thing's not so much fun this year somehow and it's so cold and ...' Barbara looked at her daughter sympathetically. She could imagine where this change of mood had come from.

'Of course Lena, you're missing Kim, hmm? It's not the same, is it? Today's not as busy as usual, I'll manage.'

Lena sighed, 'Thanks Mami, you're right, somehow or other everything's just,' she paused, 'pointless.'

Barbara grinned,

'Yeah yeah, it'll work out all right. Tomorrow you'll be out with your dad. You'll find other things to think about.'

3. A Surprise at the Airfield

On Sunday morning at Moorbach airfield, Lena was freezing. She had now been standing beside a Cessna, a small single engine aircraft, in the hangar for half an hour. She was bored and the shoptalk about planes and engines irritated her. It was her day, what was going on?

'We'll just drop in quickly, I have to give these papers to a friend.' Dad had said on the way to the airfield. He had picked her up in the morning at home as agreed and then treated her to breakfast at the Waldcafé. Jakob had stayed home under protest. After breakfast they had gone to the airfield.

Lena was still in a bad mood about Isabella. Of course she had called Kim straight away yesterday afternoon and told her everything. Kim had been upset too, but said she wanted to answer Philipp's email as if nothing had happened and not mention it. They had both thought that was the smartest move.

'He'll find out soon enough what a cow she is,' Kim had said. She'd sounded more dejected than self-assured as she said it though.

Lena was correspondingly pensive and uncommunicative today. Her father came to terms with that cheerfully enough, however. They had cinema tickets for the afternoon.

'I'll just go and look around outside,' she called to the men, who were leaning under the wing and tinkering with something or other.

'Yeah yeah, I'll be finished in a moment,' answered her father absent-mindedly.

Lena stepped back outside the hangar door. It was a wonderful clear day with puffy white clouds, but she still found it quite cold and windy. Outside the hangar was a huge asphalted area. On the edge of the asphalt were two fuel pumps for filling the planes. Further away behind the pumps, near the airfield entrance was another large hangar. Its doors were wide open, and it was mostly empty. There were only two planes, right at the back. An asphalt path for the planes ran between the areas in front of each hangar towards the runway. That was why they had walked around the outside of the hangar for safety earlier. Beside the other hangar there was a kind of kiosk or clubhouse. Lena wasn't sure if she could walk straight over or had to go around the outside again. The warning signs had been only outside the airfield, but she was inside now, wasn't she? She couldn't see anything anywhere. From somewhere behind the hangar she could hear engine noises.

For a couple more minutes, Lena stood around feeling uncertain. Just as she was about to muster her courage and simply march over, a completely rusted out, ancient hatchback car shot around the corner with its motor screaming. Lena took a step backwards, shocked. The car pulled up at the pumps with a tyre chirp. Then the engine stalled. The old car hopped forward one last time and then came to a stop. The driver's door opened and to Lena's infinite astonishment, a tall lanky boy with brown hair, glasses and a thousand pimples sprang out: Philipp's best friend, Martin.

Martin waved to her a little awkwardly. He was red in the face.

'Hi Lena! What are you doing here? Cool wheels, hey? I haven't quite got the hang of changing down yet, the brakes are so old, we're not really supposed to go so fast...'

'Martin, are you mad? You're not allowed to drive a car alone!

What are you doing?' replied Lena indignantly, still a little shocked. She walked over to Martin and the car. A strange looking contraption was fitted to the roof: a heavy metal bar with two hooks, one on the left and one on the right. 'What is THAT thing?' she asked, curious in spite of herself, and added: 'Oh yeah, hello, I'm here with my father, he's tinkering with something or other with a friend in the hangar and won't finish.' In the meantime Martin had started fuelling up the car. Lena looked on. She was quite impressed.

'Oh, we all have to be able to drive here or we'd never get anywhere, you know? Retrieving cables, launch point bus and so on. It's private land after all, it's allowed. And they're all only old bombs – this is our Lepo,' said Martin. Lena didn't understand a word.

'Your what? What are you all doing here anyway?'

'Gliding of course, what do you think? We tow out the winch cables with the Lepo[1] here, we have to get off the ground somehow – and it's called a *Lepo* just because it's Opel backwards, you know, the brand of car,' grinned Martin, hanging the hose back on the fuel pump.

'YOU can fly?' Lena couldn't help being astonished. 'You're only fourteen, is that possible? Is Philipp here too? I always thought you played football,' she asked, wide-eyed.

'Ah don't be silly, you know Philipp has nothing in his head but football,' replied Martin.

'I thought you both…' said Lena.

'Nah,' Martin cut in, 'not really, I'm not so fast, and anyway…'

---

[1] You can find explanations of aeronautical details at the back of the book!

He blushed again and was silent for a moment, then he set about explaining, 'I'm learning. I fly with an instructor in a two-seater. I've been allowed to fly since autumn last year when I turned 14. It's so cool.'

'For real?' Lena was lost for words. Somehow she wouldn't have thought Martin was capable of doing anything like that. He was in his element.

'Do you want to come to the launch point?' he asked excitedly, 'I'll show you everything. Your dad will need a while yet for sure, Lima Zulu has been out of service for ages…'

'Um…' Lena didn't understand everything he'd said, 'OK, I'll just quickly ask.' She flitted back into the Hangar. The men were still discussing the problem.

Her father thought it was a great idea.

'I'll follow you in a little while.'

When Lena came back out, Martin had already started the engine.

'Are you really sure you know what you're doing?' she asked dubiously as she got in. Martin grinned and set off.

The launch point was at the other end of the airfield.

'Why don't you take off from the asphalt runway right in front of the Hangars?' asked Lena, 'wouldn't that be more practical?'

'Then we'd be launching to the East,' explained Martin, 'from Zero Niner, that's what that runway direction's called, that means on a heading of 090 degrees if you imagine the points of a compass. But aircraft always have to take off into the wind, otherwise they won't develop the proper lift. Today we have a west wind, so we're taking off on a heading of 270 degrees, from runway Two Seven. Understand? And we often launch the gliders from the grass runway – after landing it always takes a while to push the glider back with the others, on the grass we don't block the asphalt runway for the power planes.'

'Ah-ha, I get it! Now I understand. I've never really thought about it – did you learn all that here?' Lena was amazed.

'I've always thought flying was fantastic,' answered Martin, 'and you can learn everything here. We've got four gliding instructors in the club, so usually one has time to train with us at weekends. In winter there's theory lessons once a week and you have to practice for the radio licence too. We maintain our own gliders as well, the weather's too cold anyway and there's no thermals.'

'No what?' Lena couldn't keep up – he seemed to know such a lot about it…

'Thermals – rising air masses, for example when the sun heats up the ground in a field and the ground heats the air above it. Then the warm air rises – that rising air mass is the thermal. You try to find thermals like that in the glider. Then you circle in them, climb with the air to gain height and once you've got the height, you can glide on. You have to work your way from one thermal to the next to get along.'

'Wow – that sounds pretty complicated. So how do you know when you've go to the top? It sounds a bit like a lift. And what if you don't find any thermals?' marvelled Lena.

'Oh you can see that, you have a vario in the cockpit, it tells you: zero lift. Good pilots can feel it anyway, in their behind so to speak. And if you don't find anything, you have to land. Back at the airfield if you're not too far away, or in a field if you are. But you should only fly further away when the weather's right!' Martin warmed to his subject. He was really proud to be able to explain everything to Lena.

4. At the Launch Point

They had arrived at the launch point, where the gliders took off. A couple of cars were parked a few hundred metres further along the asphalt runway from the hangars, near the trees. In front of the cars were a camping table and a few chairs under a beach umbrella. Three gliders were waiting to one side, parallel to the runway. The two at the back had one wing tip weighed down with an old tyre. Several people were standing and sitting around the table. Two men were sitting in the front glider. A boy who might have been about Martin's age stood at the wing tip and seemed to be waiting for something to happen. He had just put his free arm up in the air vertically. Martin brought the car to a stop and managed to stall the engine again.

'Oops, sorry. We're here,' he announced, 'come on!' They got out and walked towards the table. At that moment the glider moved and the boy at the wing tip started to run. The glider picked up speed amazingly quickly and the boy let go of the wing. After only a few metres the glider shot up into the air almost vertically. Only now did Lena see that there was a rope hanging from underneath the glider. The other end must have been somewhere at the other end of the airfield.

'Cool,' said Lena in amazement, 'does it always go up so steeply?' The glider climbed into the sky like a kite on a string. When it had apparently gone as high as it could on the rope, it tipped forward into a normal flight attitude and the rope fell back to the ground, getting shorter all the way.

'That's a winch launch, the winch pulls in the cable and the glider climbs till the cable gets released at the highest point. It looks dramatic, but you get used to it pretty quickly. That was our two-seater, the good old 21, it's our trainer, an ASK-21.'

'Martin, there you are, will you retrieve the cables? Oh – you've brought a visitor! Hello, I'm Marianne.' A young woman came towards her and offered Lena her hand.

'This is Lena, from my class at school,' Martin introduced her. 'Her father's working on Lima Zulu with Mikey, out the back.'

'Yeah that can take some time,' laughed Marianne.

'Come with me to the launch table Lena, Martin will be back in a minute. Have you been to a gliding field before?'

'No, never,' answered Lena, following her. Martin climbed back into the Lepo and belted away, this time along the grass runway.

'Come on boys, make room, we've got a visitor – this is Lena, a school friend of Martin's, she'll be watching us for a while.' Marianne sat down. On the table in front of her sat an antiquated telephone, a two-way radio and a couple of lists. She pointed to the chair beside her. A tall, grey-haired, extremely thin man was just getting up from it.

'Hello,' Lena nodded to the group in general.

'And good day to you... now let's see here,' the grey-haired man shook her hand. 'I'm Piet and this is Stefan, Karl, Bolle and Markus – but you don't need to remember their names, they can't.' He winked at her.

The boys mumbled some greeting or other and started pushing the second glider onto the runway.

'I'm Lena, my father is out the back in the hangar with Mike...' began Lena, by way of explaining her sudden appearance.

'No! You're SMALL PAUL's kid? Well, it's about time he brought you along! I've known your dad for twenty-five years; he came here to learn to fly back then. Hasn't been here for ages – always the same when they grow up, no time, no time... oh yeah...' Piet was really pleased and was still gripping Lena's hand.

'Look out Lena, you can prepare yourself for a long story now,' grinned Marianne. 'When old Piet gets going there's no stopping him.'

'Why is he called SMALL Paul?' asked Lena curiously.

'Back then, we had two Pauls in the club and your father was a pipsqueak 14-year-old when he started – he always had to fly with lead weights or the centre of gravity wouldn't have been right. So he picked up the name pretty quickly, and he kept it too when he got bigger.' Piet had let go of Lena's hand and sat down on the other side of the table. The Lepo came back into view along the grass runway.

'Look, Martin's back with the winch cables,' said Marianne. The Lepo drove up the grass runway and stopped just in front of the glider. A cable hung from each side of the roof. At the other end of the airfield, Lena could just make out a kind of truck. Attached to the truck were two drums with the rest of the cables wound on to them. Apparently that was the winch.

'What's that hanging on the ends of the cables?' asked Lena.

'Parachutes,' explained Marianne, 'otherwise the cable would fall to earth much too quickly after we release, and the winch wouldn't have time to roll it up properly.'

'Have you ever flown in a glider with your father?' enquired Piet. Lena shook her head.

'No, I didn't even know he flew gliders, it never came up.'

'I don't think Paul's still actively involved,' said Marianne, 'what with the shift work in his job he really wouldn't have much time for the club at the weekends any more. And he surely hasn't got a private plane hidden away anywhere either...?'

'No, definitely not,' confirmed Lena.

'Well then Lena, it's about time young lady!' exclaimed Piet, laughing. 'What do you say to us two good-looking types taking a turn together?'

'What? I don't understand...' At first Lena didn't know what he meant. Then the penny dropped.

'Oh, you mean in the glider? Can we really fly, just like that?' She was wide-eyed again.

'Well, Lena, in a few moments our 21 will be back, then we'll sit you in and off we go! You have never sat in a glider and that state of affairs must not be allowed to continue. It will be my honour, young lady. And I'll let your father know what I think of his negligence later.'

'Piet, you don't miss a trick, do you?' Marianne chided him, 'she might not even want to fly. Leave her to just sit and watch what we do here for a while in her own time.' Then, turning deftly to Lena, 'but if you really would like to – Piet is our oldest and best instructor. You really can get in with him anytime without thinking twice. Oh wait – the K8's ready.'

In the meantime, one of the gliders was now ready to fly. Martin had attached one of the cables to it and was driving the Lepo around behind the launch table. The other boys stood behind the glider and one had taken up position at the wingtip. Marianne reached for the radio:

'Moorbach Info, a glider launch.'

'Launch area clear,' came the crackling answer.

Now Marianne picked up the telephone handset and turned a

crank handle on the phone body where the keypad should have been with her other hand.

'Right, we've got the K8 on the north cable ready to launch.'

'So, how's it going?' Martin sat down next to Lena.

'Take up slack,' directed Marianne over the phone. The cable started to move forwards slowly in the grass. 'All out! All out!' The glider rolled forwards and the boy started to run again. The glider was in the air in a moment. Everyone watched the launch until the cable was released. Marianne put down the phone.

The cable sailed back towards the winch under its parachute, the rotating drum on the truck pulling it in.

'Those are the winch launch commands, our Maxl's driving the winch today, the commands tell him when to put on the power and so on,' Marianne explained.

'Well? Have you thought about it?' asked Piet.

'Thought about what?' Martin wanted to know.

'Well, actually, I think I'd really like to have a go,' said Lena tentatively.

'Well that's settled then, Lena. It looks like there might already be a few bubbles, thermals you understand, with a bit of luck we can stay up for a while,' beamed Piet.

'You're flying with Piet? I should have known. Leave them alone together for two minutes – you would never have done that with me,' quipped Martin.

'Ah, but you're not Paul's daughter. Why don't you run along and help the others push the 21 back?' retorted Piet. The larger glider had landed, and the other boys were already helping to push.

'Yes Sir!' Martin saluted with a laugh and hurried away.

'You've always got to keep those boys busy or they only get up to no good,' said Piet with a twinkle in his eye. 'Come on Lena, we have to tell Fritz he's having a break now.'

A younger man wearing a white sun hat and a parachute was walking alongside the glider as it was being pushed back.

'Fritz, take a break from circuits! I've got a guest here to fly,' Piet called to him.

'In that case…' Fritz shed the parachute and walked towards them.

'Thank you my friend,' Piet accepted the parachute and pulled it on directly.

Lena was shocked.

'Is it that dangerous, that we have to wear parachutes?' she asked.

'Nah, they're only really important when you leave the training area and fly cross country and thermal with lots of other gliders. Then you can get really close to the others – and faster than you'd like, so it's nice to have one with you,' Piet attempted to reassure her.

Lena wasn't quite convinced, but she didn't want to chicken out now. The two-seater had arrived back at the launch point and Martin helped her on with the parachute.

'Martin, would you get the lead for us please? Lena takes after her father, we'll need to pack in some extra weight,' said Piet grinning. Then he briefly explained the cockpit and the various handles, buttons and levers. By now, Lena was so excited, she couldn't take anything in – most important was where she could hang on and what she shouldn't touch at all. Martin bolted the lead into the cockpit floor and then Lena could get in. Piet was already sitting in the back, putting on his harness. Martin helped her do the harness up. There was not only a lap belt, but also shoulder harnesses and a middle strap between the legs.

'So, Lena, sitting comfortably? Nothing pinching? You can hang on here for the launch or just grab your shoulder harness – the first time is pretty exciting. And in case you need it later – there's a sick bag here in the pocket,' explained Martin considerately.

'Don't put the girl off Martin, she's got pilot's genes, she'll cope. Let's go! Close the canopy!' ordered Piet.

Martin closed the canopy and locked it. Lena heard Marianne making the radio call. Her heart fluttered.

'Everything OK, Lena?' asked Piet once more, to be sure. Lena only nodded. She had a lump in her throat and couldn't say anything. Everything was going unbelievably fast now. She looked forwards and couldn't really see the cable in the grass. The wing tip was lifted up. Martin gave her a thumbs-up and grinned encouragingly.

Out of the corner of her eye she saw her father arrive at the launch point. She was just about to wave when the glider sprang forward, accelerated and before Lena knew what was happening to her, she was pressed firmly into her seat and couldn't see anything but sky. She held on tight to her shoulder harness and instinctively wanted to keep her head down. It felt like she couldn't move at all.

'Don't worry Lena, you'll see more in a moment and the pressure will ease up,' promised Piet from the back. Sure enough, after a little while, the glider's nose was lowered, the loud wind noise of the launch dropped off and the earth came back into view. Lena could see Moorbach and the surrounding forests and fields from above. Then there was a sharp jolt as Piet released the cable.

5. Gliding? Gliding!

It was suddenly wonderfully still and peaceful. Piet had put the glider into a gentle right-hand turn and the noise had died down. Lena let go of her shoulder harness and looked around curiously.

'It's wonderful. And so peaceful,' she marvelled.

'Yeah, it's pretty different to going on holidays in an airliner,' said Piet. 'I'll just gently circle here for a while. We're in weak lift; maybe we can get a bit of height. If the turning makes you feel ill, let me know!'

Lena was simply loving it. She felt so close to everything. Piet was right. She had taken flights on holidays with Barbara or Paul, but then you were up so high so quickly – here she had a much better view of everything. For a couple of minutes, no one said anything. Piet gave her time to just look around and made a few turns to the right and left. After a while Lena actually did have the feeling that they had gained a little height.

'Is it working? Are we higher now?' she asked.

'Yes, you can see for yourself, your altimeter is in the middle of the panel. It's showing a little over five, which means we're now at over 500 metres. We had about 350 metres when we released. You can tap the panel beside the instrument gently. Usually the reading corrects itself a bit.' Lena tapped the instrument panel and the needle jumped to 5.1 – so that would be 510 metres. Now Piet flew a bit further away from the airfield, making a few full turns to the right or left every now and then. It began to get noticeably colder in the cockpit. Lena was glad she had her heavy jacket on.

'How do you know where to find the thermals, Piet?' Lena wanted to know.

'When the warm air rises, it eventually cools down and the moisture in the air condenses and forms clouds – so called cumulus clouds. We've got exactly that happening today – I try to find the up-draughts under the clouds. Sometimes they're off to one side a bit because of the wind, or not even there at all if there's too much wind. If you want, you can come onto the controls with me and feel what's going on – put your feet on the pedals and your hand on the stick. Really gently! Don't worry, nothing bad will happen.' Lena did what he said and carefully moved with the controls feeling the control inputs. Right turns, left turns, the stick and pedals moved right and left… after a while she was concentrating so much that she didn't notice the altitude anymore.

'So,' said Piet suddenly. They were flying straight. 'That's enough; we have to stay clear of the clouds. We've got almost 1,000 metres now.' Sure enough, the altimeter needle had gone right around the dial and was nearly back to zero. One full turn on the altimeter showed 1,000 metres. The airfield, forest and fields weren't nearly so close up anymore. On the contrary: Lena felt she was incredibly small in an endless sky. She didn't have time to think about that though.

'So, Lena, very gently push the stick forwards. Nothing can go wrong, I'm with you on the controls.' Lena swallowed.

'OK…' She grasped the stick more tightly and pushed it forwards, away from herself.

'Look at the horizon Lena… what happens? The glider nose drops, and the horizon comes up. The wind noise gets louder, and we fly faster. Just like that. Great. And now… carefully… pull the stick back, before we speed up too much. You're doing great. Now the nose rises and the horizon drops down and we fly slower, like so. We shouldn't fly any slower than that. Now ease the stick forwards again, nose down, till we get a normal view of the horizon again. Take note of where the horizon sits above the instrument panel! See, the glider is perfectly trimmed, and the air is calm here. You can let go of everything and nothing will happen at all. The glider just flies on.' Lena held her hands in the air.

'Look around at me, I'm not touching the controls either,' Piet waved at her. 'So, do that a few more times: fast, slow, nose down, nose up – I'm with you on the controls. Don't worry!' Lena flew like a dolphin diving – nose up, nose down, nose up, nose down and laughed.

'This is fun!'

'Is that so?' chuckled Piet, 'and now move the stick and rudder together to the right – yes, just like that… and now back to a neutral position again… perfect! Notice how the nose gradually dips? Pull back a bit and hold it up! When the string in front of you points back along the centre line, like now, we're flying straight in the air flow. If we're slipping or skidding it points diagonally off to the side. We don't want that, we'll lose too much height. The yaw string is one of your most important instruments.'

Lena had been wondering the whole time what that string was for. It was a short length of yarn taped to the outside of the canopy directly in front of her with a little piece of tape. So that was the secret, even if she hadn't quite understood the bit about slipping or skidding. She assumed it must be true, whatever it was. They flew right turns and left turns. Piet explained what she had to do to keep the string in the middle.

'And always keep the horizon looking good – like sooo, just right, then the airspeed will be right too. Now another right turn if you please – notice how it's lifting us up? Keep turning right and watch the horizon… and the yaw string!' They kept flying like that. Piet directed, and she followed his instructions.

Lena's cheeks were red, and her hands were sweaty, but she was totally concentrated on what she was doing. When Piet went quiet for a while in the turn and then abruptly said something into the radio, she was quite startled. She had been so busy with the controls, horizon and yaw string, she'd completely tuned out the chatter on the radio. She simply hadn't noticed the ground station calling them.

'So, Lena, now you can fly us back to the airfield! We've been in the air over an hour now; the others want a go at the thermals too,' said Piet.

'Really, is it that long already? I didn't notice. How time flies! It's to the left isn't it?' Lena started a turn to the left.

'Yep, that's right – I can easily believe you forgot about everything else, you wouldn't be the first. You really like this don't you?' Piet was delighted. He couldn't see from the back, but Lena was beaming.

'Oh yeah, I really feel good up here; it's soooo awesome!'

'And you are really good at it too, young lady. I haven't touched the controls or interfered at all for ten minutes. You're flying this thing on your own.'

'Really?' Lena couldn't take it in; she had assumed that Piet was still on the controls in the back. She felt flushed with pride and was really pleased.

'Like I said, pilot's genes! So, now we're nearly there; I'll take over again. Look out, now we can really put the nose down. Yahoo!' With these words Piet pulled out the air brakes.

Lena had let go of everything.

With one more zippy turn he brought them into the landing pattern.

'Delta four six downwind,' he announced on the radio.

'Roger four six. Wind two eight zero degrees, six knots,' came the reply. Lena's tension eased off as they rapidly prepared to land, but she did still feel a little uneasy in the stomach. She had flown a plane, herself, with her own hands. She would have to write to Kim as soon as she got home, no, better yet, tell her straight away on the phone.

They were already back on the ground. The ASK21 jolted and rumbled quite a lot as it rolled over the grass runway. After a few metres they came to a standstill. Her father, Martin and two of the other boys came over from the side to help push the glider back. Paul Reisenberg opened the glider canopy for Lena and helped her get out. He was beaming; he smiled at least as much as Lena.

'Of course you know we're going to miss the movie. I thought you two had set off to fly 300K's cross country.'

'Oh no! I completely forgot' cried Lena feeling quite disconcerted. She peeled off the parachute unassisted.

'Papi, Piet let me fly the glider, heaps. And in the end I was flying it by myself. It was so incredibly cool!'

'Small Paul himself, nice to see you. But it wasn't very nice of you to keep this talent here away from us for so long. She's really got the knack. You should work on it with her.' Piet had also dug himself out of the glider and thumped Paul on the shoulder. The men greeted each other heartily and embraced.

'Wow, Lena,' Martin ran over to her, 'you were gone for ages. How was it? Did old Piet let you fly? Of course he did, didn't he?' The words bubbled up out of her as she excitedly reported every detail.

They pushed the 21 back to the launch point along with the other boys and Paul. Piet walked alongside casually and chatted with Paul all the while.

6. New Plans

Lena and Paul stayed at the airfield for a while longer. Martin was next up and flew with Fritz, the other instructor. Lena sat next to Marianne and watched. One of the women had brought coffee and a huge pile of cake, so they ate and drank and chatted with Piet for a while.

It was quiet at the launch point now. The two single seaters had also found thermals and stayed up for longer. The boys who had pushed the glider back set off again. Martin was on final approach. He was practicing take offs and landings and would be launching several times in quick succession.

'Oh, that'll be a long landing,' remarked Marianne, as the 21 sailed past them rather too high.

'Yeah – and not just one, from the way he's playing with the air brakes,' grinned Piet. The glider touched down one, two, three times before it stayed on the ground and rolled to a stop.

'Lena, we're planning a little gliding camp here in the spring holidays if the weather's right,' Piet continued. 'Would you be interested in coming along? Your father told me you'll be fourteen in two weeks – that fits perfectly, you'll be old enough. The club has a special trial offer to encourage young people to join up. Maybe gliding could be for you?'

'Oh… my friend Kim's coming from Berlin in the spring holidays. She just moved there…' Lena responded.

'Maybe your friend might like to come too? The more the merrier at a gliding camp, then it really gets going. We camp out here, in tents; have barbeques every night – and what about you Paul? Not into taking a few launches again?' Piet liked the idea more and more. Paul laughed and held his hands up defensively.

'C'mon Piet, I do have to work occasionally too. Thanks, but no. The girls can think it over for themselves. It's all a bit short notice after all. They'd have to get their aviation medicals before then and so on.' Then, turning to Lena, 'that, I'd be happy to help you with. Only if Barbara agrees of course – but whether Kim's parents are that enthusiastic? We'll just have to wait and see, hmm?'

They watched Martin do three more take offs and landings, then Paul said they really had to leave. Lena said goodbye to Piet and Marianne.

'We're packing up soon too, we'll just wait for the single seaters, then we'll push everything back in the hangar. Well, till next time Lena; we might see each other again soon. Goodbye Paul!' Piet waved to them cheerfully as Lena and Paul walked along beside the trees towards the car park. Unfortunately Martin was in the air again just when they left, but Lena would see him the next day at school anyway.

The next morning when she got on the school bus, Martin was already waiting for her. He was holding some booklets and waved her over to sit with him. Lena slid into the seat next to him.

'Hi Martin.'

'Hello, I've got something for you. Did you get our club brochures yesterday? Piet said you might come to the gliding camp, is that right?'

'I'd really like to and my parents are OK with it too,' Lena responded. 'Only Kim's not so keen on flying and actually I'm supposed to be seeing her in the spring break. I don't know how it's all going to work out yet. Whatever happens I'm coming, with my mother and everyone, at Easter to check it out again. What have you got there? Let's see it.' Martin gave her the club brochure and another blue booklet.

'That's the gliding operations manual, you can have a look at it, but everything's on the net anyway under German Aero-club,' explained Martin hurriedly. 'Then you'll know all about what a circuit is and some other stuff.'

'Hey Martin, what's up?' Philipp had just got on and was looking quizzically at Lena and Martin, who had their heads together engrossed in the booklets.

'Is he babbling flying stories at you, Lena? My sympathies,' he added disparagingly with a glance at the club brochure. 'He tried that on me once too. If you don't watch out, you'll be listening to a lecture on clouds from Mr Know-it-all here in a moment.' Philipp dropped into a window seat in the row behind them and draped his legs nonchalantly over the next seat. Two first-years who had wanted to get past turned around uncertainly and found spots further forwards. Martin blushed.

'Lena was at the airfield yesterday and had a flight and she's probably coming to our gliding camp too,' he defended himself.

'Oh terrific, now we'll have two smarty pants head-in-the-clouds' rambling on about thermals and lift,' groaned Philipp.

'Ah, let him talk,' Lena tried to reassure Martin. Then she turned to Philipp, 'But you're just the coolest right? You and all your football friends. I don't run you down.'

Martin started to defend himself.

'I've got something to say to you, I…'

At that moment Isabella got on and came towards them. She swept Philipp along with her to a seat further back on the bus.

'I… but…' Martin glared after them furiously. 'Just once! If I could just think up a snappy reply when that happens, just once, … he's such a big headed idiot!'

'I know the feeling,' sighed Lena. Oh – brilliant, she thought to herself. She wondered if Kim would ever react like that to her talking about her hobby. She listened to Martin explaining on about circuits, thermals and cross-country flights and tried to ignore the couple at the back of the bus, who had now started smooching.

The last week of school before the holidays was crammed full. There were two more tests to sit. The teachers didn't seem to care that the break was starting soon and gave out piles of homework. Lena was quite absorbed in her new plans and couldn't concentrate. She found it really hard to apply herself to her schoolwork. In the breaks between classes and on the bus she tried to remember as much as she could of what Martin had told her. She wanted to impress Barbara and Johannes with her new knowledge when they went back to the airfield. Apart from that, the whole subject was uncharted territory for her and the more she learned, the more enthused she became. She wanted to know all about everything. More than once, someone had to say her name several times before she reacted when she was dreamily staring out the window at the clouds.

Philipp never missed an opportunity to rile Martin and Lena and they did their best to ignore him. Isabella, on the other hand, restrained herself from making stupid comments. She didn't ask any questions either though, despite sitting next to Lena in class and having ample opportunity had she wanted to. Lena didn't hear anything from Kim either, but she was way too busy to worry about that.

The Easter holidays finally arrived! On the Sunday morning, Barbara, Johannes, Jakob and Lena were already making their way to the airfield. It had still been raining on Saturday and they had been forced to delay their visit. Lena had skulked around the house impatiently the whole day like a tiger in a cage, incessantly peering at the sky to see if the rain clouds might clear.

Sunday morning was clear and sunny however, and they could finally begin. They arrived at the airfield at nine o'clock. A large collection of machines and aircraft was strewn around the asphalt in front of the hangar. People were pushing gliders out of the hangar and checking them over. The winch, the Lepo and an old van loaded with tables, folding chairs and umbrellas, were parked beside the car park. A couple of power planes were sitting to one side on the grass. Two gliders on the edge of the taxiway were waiting to be towed out to the launch point. Their canopies were open and the pilots were checking that everything was in good order and ready to use. In the hangar another glider hanging from the roof on ropes was being carefully let down with a chain block. Three people were standing underneath ready to grab it when it came in reach and push it out.

Lena kept a lookout for Martin, but she couldn't see him anywhere. Instead, Marianne emerged from the hangar and came over to them.

'Hello Lena, how nice to see you! And this must be your mother?' They shook hands. The adults exchanged greetings and introduced themselves. Jakob tried to climb up on the winch.

'Leave that alone!' Lena admonished him. 'You can't just climb on things, this isn't a playground.' They watched as more gliders came out of the hangar. Two older men were pushing a plane out. One was steering at the wing tip and the other pushed down on the glider nose, lifting the tail wheel off the ground. Without pushing the nose down the glider couldn't be turned in various directions because the wheels that make up a glider's undercarriage are fixed straight ahead and not steerable. As the fuselage turned, the man on the wing lowered the tip intending to lift the other wing over the winch. The wingtip whirled in an arc towards Lena, who was still standing beside the winch with Jakob.

'Look out, it's going to hit!' called Lena, thinking quickly, and just in time too.

Marianne leapt around and caught the wing tip at the last moment just before the leading edge would have crashed into the winch.

'Can't you watch what you're doing?' Marianne chided them indignantly, 'or better yet just wait two minutes till we can all push it out together? But no… always in a hurry. If Lena hadn't been here we'd be spending this beautiful day in the workshop.'

They positioned the glider gingerly alongside the other two. The men were just as shaken as Marianne and mumbled a sheepish apology.

'Thanks kid!' one of them called to Lena.

'Yes indeed, thanks a lot Lena!' added Marianne, coming back to them. 'As you can see, gliding is teamwork every moment of the day. Lucky you were on the ball.'

'Good save!' said a friendly voice behind Lena unannounced. A tall boy with freckles, brown eyes and a tousled shock of red hair was walking towards them from the car park. He tapped Lena on the shoulder, winked at her and continued on to the launch point bus where he dropped his backpack.

'Oh Maxl, give a hand over there with the ASW19 if you would, otherwise we'll never get it in the air in one piece today with our pensioners on the rampage…' Marianne entreated him.

'I want to show our guests here around a bit.'

'*Anything for you,*' answered Maxl, glancing at Lena with a grin and trotting off towards the glider.

Lena's heart missed a beat. She had seen him before sometimes at school, one or two years above her maybe. She watched him go as Marianne got them underway for a tour of the clubhouse, hangar and tower.

One of the men was sitting in the ASW19, operating the controls. Maxl was standing outside the glider, concentrating on checking the control surfaces.

'Is Martin not here today?' Lena asked Marianne.

'With all that rain yesterday it was a workshop day – I don't know how he managed it, but Martin jammed his hand dreadfully in the tool cupboard – he might not be so mobile yet… he does things like that all the time, such a klutz.'

Marianne showed them the little tower first. The controller sipped contentedly on his coffee. There was nothing going on yet. From the cabin on top of the tower they could easily see the winch driving up to one end of the grass runway with the Lepo close behind. The convoy of gliders behind the launch point bus was underway in the opposite direction. A two-seater was coupled to the bus with a tow bar. A temporary wheel was attached to one wing, so it wouldn't drag on the ground. The other gliders were being pushed by hand, which made the whole convoy rather slow.

Next they had a look at the clubhouse, a large room with several tables, lots of aircraft photos, a blackboard and a small kitchen with a homely counter. A long passageway led past the toilets, showers and a storeroom. At the end of the passage was the workshop with a connecting door to the hangar.

The hangar was almost empty. Except for two delicate-looking old gliders still hanging from the roof and an old touring motor glider in the darkest corner at the back, all the aircraft had been taken out.

Marianne patiently explained every aspect of gliding training to Barbara and Johannes, and of course Lena listened intently too. They had already been given a stack of enrolment forms.

When they stepped out of the hangar again there was another surprise in store for them.

'Papa! What are you doing here?' Lena flew into Paul's arms.

'Hi everybody, hello my little one! I thought I'd drop by and offer my support in case your Mama was having second thoughts and felt afraid for her baby. I may not have a gliding licence anymore, but I'm still allowed to drive the old Cessna. What if you go back to the launch point with Marianne for a while and I kidnap the rest of the family for a little joy flight?'

'Super-duper,' cried Jakob almost involuntarily as he jumped for joy. 'Can I sit in the front with you Paul? Pleeeease!' he begged.

'Oh, I think we can manage that,' grinned Paul. 'Shall we?' Barbara and Johannes must have known about the plan in advance, or at any rate they didn't seem very surprised.

Jakob was so excited, there was no holding him back. Lena was pretty happy about the idea too. It meant she didn't have to turn up at the launch point like a little girl with her parents holding her hand. It was so much better this way.

Once Mama and Johannes see how cool flying is, they won't be so worried anymore either, she thought. Perfect.

Marianne and Lena headed off for the launch point and the others climbed into the Cessna for their joy flight. When they were about half way there, the Cessna caught up with them as it taxied towards the asphalt runway, and everybody waved happily.

In his excitement, Jakob nearly knocked the sunglasses off Paul's nose as he waved. Lena had a good view of their take off as they strolled on.

7. Driving the Bus

The first pair of winch cables was just being towed out as Lena and Marianne got to the launch point. Marianne wanted to fly a couple of circuits in the relative quiet of the morning. That would leave the two-seater free, for the younger student pilots to fly the pants off it in the thermals later in the day. She hadn't flown much since her baby was born and wanted to ease back in to it slowly. Her husband was going to come to the airfield with their baby in the middle of the day.

'Come and help me with the parachute, Lena, and get someone to show you how to hook on… just watch what goes on, help with pushing back – you won't be bored will you?' Lena held up the parachute, so Marianne could put it on more easily. Bolle, one of the boys she had met last time, came over and showed her how she could help Marianne prepare for the flight. Then Marianne closed the canopy and gave the thumbs up.

'Ready for rope?' asked Bolle.

'Ready for rope!' Marianne responded. Bolle and Lena kneeled beside the glider belly.

'Open!' Bolle called out. Marianne pulled the release handle, the beak in the belly release opened and Bolle hooked on the cable.

'Close!' The beak closed again. Lena and Bolle moved off to the side. Maxl was already standing at the wing tip for the launch.

A minute later the glider was in the air. Maxl came over to them.

'Hi, I'm Maxl. Are you a new member?' he asked Lena.

'This is Lena,' Bolle introduced her.

'Hello, no… yes… maybe – well… I might be able to come to the gliding camp, and then I'll have to see,' stammered Lena, annoyed with herself all the while that she was suddenly so nervous.

'Yeah, that's fantastic – come on, we're pushing the K8 out.' Maxl brought her along to the single seater that was standing off to the side.

They pushed the glider out together.

'Don't you two know each other from school?' asked Bolle. 'Lena's in the same class as Martin.'

'Really? Did Martin sign you up?' asked Maxl grinning.

'Nah, just coincidence, my father used to fly here, Paul – he's off with the rest of the family in the Cessna right now.' Lena was a bit miffed that Maxl hadn't recognized her. Bolle held the parachute up for Maxl.

'Ah, let Lena do it Bolle, we'll manage, won't we Lena?' grinned Maxl. Lena tried hard to get everything right, just as Bolle had shown her, but he stayed with her and double-checked everything. 'See you later then,' Maxl called after her as Bolle lifted the wing.

Once Maxl was in the air, they went off to be ready to push back Marianne's glider after she landed. She was already on final approach.

'Just you watch, Maxl will stay up for sure,' Bolle asserted. 'If anybody's got a nose for thermals, it's him – we won't see him again for a couple of hours. Such a freak!' Bolle's envy was written all over his face.

'Has he got his licence already?' asked Lena.

'No, he's not sixteen yet; you can't get it before then. He flies better than plenty of licenced pilots though. I always land back –

I've been flying just as long as Maxl, but I'm sure I've only got half the flight hours,' Bolle sighed. Lena almost felt a little sorry for him.

Marianne landed right next to them. Lena was soon busily involved in operations. There was always an instructor nearby watching whatever Bolle and the others showed her, to make sure everything stayed on track. Lena had been too busy getting gliders ready and pushing them back to notice that her family had landed again some time ago.

'Come on Lena, we'll go and pick your family up in the bus,' Marianne offered. 'They'll be wondering what you've been doing all this time for sure.'

'Oh – are they already back?' Lena wondered.

'I can see you've got stuck into it,' laughed Marianne. 'Right, in you get, you're driving!'

'What? I've never driven a car.' Lena was wide-eyed.

'Well, it's about time then! You'll get plenty of practice on the gliding camp anyway. Everyone here has to drive.'

They got into the van and Lena sat behind the wheel for the first time in her life. She knew roughly how everything worked, but she had never tried it out for herself. Marianne patiently explained all the controls to her and Lena followed her instructions step by step. Jerkily, slowly, and with much grinding of gears they drove down to the clubhouse.

Jakob was sitting on the handrail by the barbeque area slurping lemonade. When he saw who was driving the van he promptly choked and started coughing.

'Look Mama! It's not fair. I want to come to the gliding camp too! And drive cars. And learn to fly,' he demanded indignantly of his mother.

Lena stalled the engine just like Martin and brought the vehicle to a halt. They got out.

'Well?' smirked Barbara. 'It looks to me like you're hard at work learning already.' Jakob bounded around excitedly, keen to tell them all about the flight with Paul.

'Sorry Jakob, you'll have to wait a few years yet, you're still too young,' Marianne told him regretfully. 'You'll just have to come and visit your sister often when she's here.'

They drove back to the launch point together. Lena told her family about everything she had already learnt. Barbara and Johannes were impressed to see how much had soaked in over such a short time, and quite pleased with Lena's enthusiasm. Jakob was allowed to help push a couple of gliders back and or sit in the cockpit while the others pushed. At noon Marianne drove them all back to the car park, where she picked up her husband and their baby.

'Thanks a lot for showing us everything, Marianne, I'm sure Lena will have plenty of fun here,' said Barbara.

There was now nothing standing between Lena and the gliding camp. They filled out piles of forms and made their farewells.

'I'll pick you up on Thursday for your aviation medical appointment,' promised Paul. Lena would have liked to stay longer. She would have got to see how long Maxl stayed up, and driving was fun too. She would just have to be patient for a while.

After that, the Easter break dragged on interminably for Lena. Easter, and shortly afterwards her birthday, were both really nice and she felt happy, but she wasn't really that interested in celebrating.

Paul gave her a book about gliding for her birthday: *Flying*

Sailplanes – A Practical Training Manual by Helmut Reichmann. Now she had a book again, to bury herself in and pass the time. She actually longed to be back at school. She would see Martin again and might even be able to chat to Maxl...

Kim and Lena planned to see each other at the end of the spring break. That meant seeing Kim would only overlap with the gliding camp by two days. Hopefully, Kim wouldn't feel too put out. Lena fondly hoped that her friend would be able to share at least a bit of her enthusiasm.

8. Waiting... Waiting... Waiting...

There were six weeks between Easter and the spring break. School had started and Martin's hand was OK again. He was pleased that Lena was now actually registered for the gliding camp. She told him all about her last visit to the airfield and her aviation medical.

She often saw Maxl too. They said hello to each other and sometimes he winked at her conspiratorially, but to Lena's disappointment they never really talked. Maxl was usually surrounded by other boys from his class and Lena didn't dare start a conversation with him. Kim enthusiastically recommended making the first move, but that wasn't Lena's style. Maxl didn't budge either, so Lena had to be happy with friendly nods from a distance.

Lena and Kim had resumed their usual email correspondence and Lena furnished Kim with as many details as she could make out of the Isabella-Phillip relationship.

In turn, Martin kept Lena entertained with stories from the airfield. He must have ironed out his landing technique because one weekend in May the time had come. Martin had flown his first three solo flights. As pilots say: he had *earned his wings*! Martin was allowed to fly on his own! He recounted every detail of that exhilarating day many times over. When someone earned their wings, they had a large bouquet of wildflowers pressed firmly into their hands. Usually there was a prickly thistle buried in the middle of it. Later the *culprit* would be bent over the wing and every person privileged enough to have witnessed the incident would file past and give them a more or less spirited slap on the backside.

That was supposed to impart the proper feel for thermals in future flying. Martin said some of the boys hadn't been particularly subtle about it on the day. At any rate it was better to stand up for a while afterwards.

On the up side you got to proudly wear the A-Badge, a metal pin with a single set of wings. The first test on the way to your pilot's licence was behind you!

'And what happens to you later, in the other stages?' Lena was almost afraid to ask. This aspect of gliding wasn't to her liking at all. It seemed like a fairly harsh ritual to her. 'What about when you get your licence?'

'Nothing so dramatic,' Martin reassured her. 'In our club, men give up their tie or shirt collar, women a bra, and it gets hung on the back wall of the hangar. You should have a look, there's some ancient stuff hanging around in there, there must still be something from your dad. The custom's dying out though; lots of clubs don't do it anymore.'

The more time went by, the less real Lena's experiences on the airfield seemed to her. Martin's stories could have been from another world.

At first, Lena had wanted to tell Kim more about Maxl. How he had suddenly been there, standing in front of her, trusting her to help straight off... Since no direct contact had come to pass at school though, she felt a little foolish. What should she say? That he winked at her? Piet had done that too. She shouldn't flatter herself on that account.

She sometimes watched Maxl surreptitiously in the breaks when the opportunity arose. He didn't seem to have a girlfriend, at least not at school. She couldn't really tell though whether he flirted with other girls the way he did with her. She kept quiet and didn't tell Kim any of it. It was embarrassing. All the same she got butterflies every time she passed Maxl in the schoolyard.

At home Lena dug out her tent from the summer before last. The whole family had been camping at the beach in Italy. Sleeping bag, inflatable mattress, everything still there. She often read from Reichmann, but in fact she didn't get much out of it because she didn't have the practical grounding.

Jakob's new favourite game was being a pilot. He was always  running around her in screaming dives, sometimes with his friends and sometimes without. His big sister was his hero now; she was going to learn to fly soon. Lena was just irritated and stressed. 'Can't you leave me alone? I'm reading!' She snapped at him more and more often. She always felt sorry afterwards. She was just so impatient for the gliding camp to start.

The waiting seemed to drag on forever and Lena was eaten up with misgivings and self-doubt. If only Maxl had spoken to her properly. If only Kim had any interest in the airfield. As it was, she could only wait and brood.

Once or twice she saw Martin in the afternoons after school. Somehow the discussions were always a bit one-sided though. Martin was always obsessed with flying and couldn't stop retelling stories about it. It was quite interesting at first, but it did get pretty boring after a while. To top it off, he didn't seem at all interested in airfield gossip, like who did what with whom and so on. A few times they complained to each other about Philipp, who kept on teasing them as before and made out that they were girlfriend and boyfriend. That part didn't seem to worry Martin so much. He didn't know much about Philipp's relationship with Isabella either, so that subject was soon exhausted.

Eventually, the long wait came to an end. Lena packed her bag for the airfield. The week before, Paul had handed her a *bucket hat* with a grin. It was a baggy white sun hat that Lena thought made her look like a mop with a real bucket hanging on it.

'I don't have to actually wear that, do I?' she had asked her father in horror.

'Try it out,' he'd suggested with a laugh, 'if the peak on your baseball cap doesn't bother you… in my experience it's annoying every time you bash it on the canopy.' Lena had defiantly jammed her old baseball cap on the other way around, with the peak to the back. She did pack the bucket hat too though, just in case. Her father had warned her that when you spend a lot of time at the airfield, and in the air, the sun could give you a real burn.

Lena packed sunscreen, sunglasses, jeans, shorts, t-shirts, sweatshirts, underwear, socks, running shoes and assorted bits and pieces into her large backpack and maneuvered it into the hall. The tent and her other camping gear were already there. Barbara came around the corner carrying a large basket.

'Look, darling,' she pointed to the contents of the basket, 'I know you'll have food and drink and everything supplied at the airfield, but I've packed a few of your favourites.' In the basket were piles of gummy bears, biscuits, nuts, juice, assorted fruit, and right at the top, her very own phone.

Lena picked it up in amazement. Until now she had never felt any desire to have a phone. Although many of the kids at school wouldn't be seen dead without one, the trend had passed her by. She had never needed one either. Barbara and Johannes trusted her. They didn't need to know where she was every two minutes when she went into town with friends. Not that she had done anything like that very much since Kim left. Lena herself preferred talking to her friends face to face. Exchanging emails with Kim was the only exception and that was only because Kim had moved away.

'If you feel homesick or anything comes up, you can call us anytime or just send an SMS. I have to admit it's an older model. It's Johannes' old phone, but I'm sure it will do the job,' said her mother, a little self-consciously. Apparently it wasn't that easy for her to leave her big girl all stranded and alone on the airfield. Lena hugged Barbara impulsively.

'Awesome,' she exclaimed, 'now I can text Kim too! Thanks! What's my phone number?' Barbara gave her some pieces of paper with the details and passwords.

'Go easy with it, or you'll use up all your credit straight away,' she warned.

9. Gliding Camp

The weather was perfect, and it was forecast to get really hot. Johannes and Jacob helped Lena pitch her tent on the large grassy area behind the clubhouse on the edge of the car park. Several other tents, two motor homes and an old maroon coloured delivery van with a tent annex were already set up on the lawn. The back of the delivery van was covered in stickers from glider aerobatics competitions.

Martin was struggling with putting up his tent beside Lena's.

'Stupid thing!' he swore. 'When I get my licence the first thing I'm doing is buying a bus like Piet's, and that'll be the end of this boy scout rubbish.'

'I'll keep you in mind if I'm ever selling my baby,' grinned Piet, stepping out of the annex. 'Hi Lena, everything OK here? Come over to the clubhouse when you're finished, briefing's in half an hour.' On the way past he expertly nudged the tent pole that Martin had been battling with and it slipped neatly into its proper place.

'Thanks,' sighed Martin, relieved.

When Lena had stowed all her things in her tent, she said goodbye to Johannes and Jacob who were going on to the swimming hole. Barbara had to work, so Lena had already parted from her at home.

'What do I say now? Break a leg? Here's mud in your eye? Whatever, I hope you really enjoy yourself Lena. Give us a call sometime! Or if you want to have a break and spend a night at home... let us know! Otherwise, see you on Friday. We'll pick

Kim up at the station and bring her here.' Johannes gave her a firm hug and went on his way with Jakob. Lena took a deep breath. Now it was for real!

'Greetings all,' Bolle's voice rang out from behind Lena. 'Martin, is that your tent? You're not serious, are you?' Maxl and Bolle wended their way past them with broad grins. Lena immediately got butterflies again when she saw Maxl.

'Hi,' she squeaked, sounding rather pathetic in her agitation. Martin was already sweating, now he blushed.

'What's wrong with it?' he asked, annoyed.

'It'll collapse in the first puff of wind!' said Bolle snidely. Maxl nodded his agreement.

'Well, Lena's tent seems quite sturdy!' he said with a laugh. 'Martin, when yours caves in, just move in there and Lena can stay with me, I've got room. The big green one back there,' he pointed over his shoulder and winked at her.

Now it was Lena's turn to blush. She turned away to hide her flushed cheeks and pretended to tidy one last thing in the tent. The two boys walked on laughing.

'Hurry up you two; briefing starts in a moment. Glad you're here Lena.' Maxl waved as they left. Lena's heart gave a little flutter. Well that was a good start, she thought happily to herself.

Martin tinkered around cursing for a few more minutes and Lena helped him as well as she could. Then they made their way to the clubhouse. The hangar doors were still closed. Five unfamiliar glider trailers were parked to the side by the trees. Some of the owners had set up their tents and caravans beside their trailers. Two trailers were open, and Lena could make out the fuselages of the gliders waiting to be rigged. The wings were still stowed parallel to the fuselages in the trailers. A few women had made themselves comfortable on folding chairs and were enjoying coffee in the morning sun.

The clubhouse was full fit to burst. Lena sat next to Marianne, taking the last free chair. Martin went over to sit with Maxl and the other boys on the large window board.

Bolle and Maxl were grinning boisterously and Martin poked them in the ribs as he went past.

Piet extended hearty greetings to everyone and introduced all the newcomers and guests. He explained a few ground rules and procedures, then assigned the various trainees to their corresponding instructors. Apart from Lena there were two boys starting from scratch. The three of them would mainly be training with Fritz and Piet in the ASK21. There was also a tow plane available for the week. That meant that apart from winch launches, it was also possible to take an aerotow and get towed up higher or right to a thermal. Piet pointed out the special features of the airfield to the more experienced pilots and guests. Lastly, the prevailing weather conditions were discussed before everyone was dismissed.

Piet opened the hangar doors. Marianne, Martin, Maxl, Bolle and a few others immediately started carefully taking the gliders, vehicles and the winch outside. Fritz showed Lena and the other two beginners, Markus and Stefan, where the parachutes were kept. They also had to collect the batteries from the charging station. Without batteries there would be no radio or audio vario.

'The vario shows you whether the air mass around you is rising or falling. You can read it on the mechanical instrument in the cockpit. That's good enough at first. Later when you fly more cross-country, you can turn on the audio vario. Then you hear a high tone in lift and a low tone in sink. That means you can concentrate more on the airspace around you and your lookout. It's very important not to be distracted by constantly looking at the instruments, especially when you're thermalling with lots of other gliders!' Fritz lectured them.

There was an easterly wind today. That meant they didn't have to pull all the gliders up to the other end of the airfield. They could just set up the launch point directly under the little tower. The tow plane, an old Cessna 182, was already parked right in front of the tower.

They inspected their ASK21 with Fritz. Any foreign objects in the cockpit? Main pins and all control connections correctly rigged? Anything visibly cracked, broken or damaged? Battery connected correctly? There were thousands of details to check and Fritz went through everything with them point by point.

'Lena, you're up first, will you get ready please? Then we can get straight into it!' Marianne came over and helped Lena with the parachute and getting in. Before Fritz got in the back seat himself, he squatted beside the cockpit and went over all the instruments and controls, explaining their functions.

'We'll take quite a high tow behind the Cessna because there's no thermals yet. That'll give you time to practice. You can gently stay on the controls with me on the launch till we release. Piet told me you took over and flew it yourself last time. We'll go through all that again one step at a time, till you feel confident with it. If that works out well up high, after a few launches you can take the controls for the launches and landings too!'

Markus and Stefan stood next to them absorbing every word. They could hardly wait to get in the air themselves.

Behind Lena, the next two-seater was getting ready too. Aerotow, i.e. launching with a power plane, wasn't taught here that often, so the older trainees needed some catch-up training too. Lena learnt and flew, then the others had a turn. The gliders had to be pushed back; she ran here and there, hooked on ropes, helped the others, listened to lots of explanations and tried to follow all the instructions. She met a lot of different people whose names she couldn't remember yet. People gossiped, told jokes and stories, and got to know each other better. In the afternoon, when they were pushing back the 21 after Lena's sixth flight, it seemed to her like she had never done anything else. They were like a big family and everyone helped out.

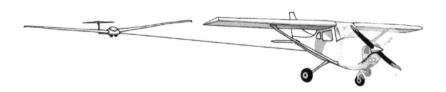

Martin couldn't get the hang of aerotow at all and simply didn't understand how Lena could actually like it better than winch launching. In fact she was a little nervous about the winch launches she was supposed to take later in the day when the thermals had died down and the air was stiller.

On her third launch Lena was allowed to take the controls and flew a kind of wild dance behind the tug. Gradually her control handling grew calmer and smoother.

After a while she managed to stay more or less under control on tow without Fritz having to take over all the time. He was very pleased with his pupil.

'You've really got the knack. Piet's right, you're a natural,' he praised Lena.

'How do you do it?' whined Martin. 'When I try it's always "too high, you're pulling the tail of the tug up, we'll fall out of the sky". Or I fly too low and get in the turbulence. The winch is much easier. Pull back once and you're done.'

'You've just got to learn to be a bit gentler Martin, you're too heavy-handed,' explained Fritz.

They pushed the 21 off to the side and helped a few single seaters push back to the launch point or the hangar after landing. Lena had no idea how many times she had now run up and down the runway. She was soaked in sweat and her skin burned. It was a very warm day and they must all have got a bit of a tan in the good weather.

'Come on Lena, we'll go and tow out the cables. You drive there, I'll drive back.' It was Maxl, waving her over. Oh no, thought Lena, I can't really drive yet. Her anxiety was groundless however. Maxl wasn't in the least overbearing and patiently showed her how to drive the Lepo.

'You see, not hard at all really, is it? If you can fly a plane, you can certainly drive a car!'

Together they hooked the cable parachutes onto the roof bars. Bolle was driving the winch and gave them the signal to set off. Maxl accelerated the Lepo and they trundled back to the launch point at a steady speed. He turned up the radio and they sang along at the top of their lungs. The windows were wide open and the wind whistled around their ears. All too soon their drive came to an end. Lena could have driven along beside Maxl like that for hours, but he had already leapt out of the Lepo and unhooked the cables.

The K8 was ready at the launch point and after that it would be Lena's turn for a winch launch.

Markus and Stefan were already waiting for her.

'Where did you go?' asked Stefan, with his mouth full. Some of the older members had organised a generous buffet for lunch. In the afternoon there were piles of cakes, muffins and drinks laid out ready. Mama really needn't have worried about the provisions, thought Lena to herself. Stefan bit into his muffin heartily.

'Mmm, you really have to try these Lena, then you won't need so much lead either.' Lena and Markus couldn't suppress a grin. Stefan wasn't exactly slim, and they had already secretly wondered whether his massive belly wasn't in the way in the cockpit. He crammed the rest of his muffin into his mouth and handed Lena the parachute.

The 21 was pushed online, Fritz came over and Lena got ready. Fritz went through the winch launch procedures with her. She would be on the controls with him. The cable was hooked on; Lena was ready to fly and gave the *thumbs up* signal. Markus lifted the wing tip. Take up slack. All out, all out.

'Hold the plane nice and flat, don't pull back like crazy straight away, Lena,' instructed Fritz from the back, 'or we'll fly a kavalierstart. If you have a cable break while you're hanging too steeply on the cable in the first 50 metres it's very dangerous. The airflow isn't established properly yet and you won't have time to get the aircraft into a landing attitude – watch – like this.' On this launch Lena noticed that they really did have control of the aircraft. Back when she had taken her first winch launch with Piet they had seemed to rocket into the sky so incredibly fast. Now she carefully followed the various phases and flight attitudes of the launch.

'Bravo! Not so scary after all, eh? Much quicker than aerotow too. Now, we're not very high and we're not in lift. You can do two circles Lena, and then we'll join downwind.' Joining downwind meant flying parallel to the runway in the opposite direction to the planned landing. It was the start of flying a circuit and allowed you to adjust the angles to the landing point and plan the landing according to the conditions. Adjustments to the flight path made in the circuit would affect the total distance flown and allow the pilot to make the turn onto final approach in a good position to make a good landing. Lena flew the ASK21 and followed her instructions as well as she could.

'Lookout, my aircraft!' Fritz suddenly took control. Lena had just straightened up on final and they were only a couple of hundred metres away from landing. She had thought everything was going well.

The K8 that had just landed was still in the middle of the grass runway, and they were heading straight for it! The pilot was getting out of the cockpit in a leisurely fashion and the crew were on the way to help him push back. Fritz put the airbrakes away with one swift movement and changed course off to the right. Now the nose was lined up on the asphalt runway.

'That can happen, Lena, especially in the evening when the thermals shut down and everyone wants to land at the same time. Always keep a good lookout! Your aircraft, you land it!'

Lena took the controls again. She groaned to herself. What else was she supposed to look out for? She was happy to finally have the plane under control and now she was supposed to look after everyone else as well? Great!

'The threshold is your aiming point, aim for that, that's good…more airbrake, full airbrake, and…now look forward to the horizon and raise the nose a little, a bit more, hold it off!'

The glider settled, touched down and rolled forwards. When they had passed the K8 and slowed down quite a lot, Fritz put in full left rudder, which steered the 21 off the asphalt runway. After a few more metres they came to a stop behind the K8.

'Please don't try taxiing like that yet! You'll learn details like those when the time's right,' he warned her directly. Lena just shook her head. She'd be quite happy just being able to land the glider without help.

10. Outlanding

By the time the gliders were washed and stowed in the hangar, the winch and Cessna were refuelled and everything else was packed away, it was almost nine o'clock in the evening.

In the camping area, the barbeque was working overtime and everyone attacked the food ravenously. Benches and tables had been set up outside. Lena sat down next to Martin and Stefan, feeling tired. She had flown nine flights for the day. Some of the trainees had flown longer flights in thermals rather than practicing circuits. All the others had flown a similar number of launches to Lena. Everyone had been fairly busy for the whole day.

On top of that she had learned so much and had so many new ideas to deal with that she was exhausted. The first thing she did was gulp down a large bottle of water.

The throng around the barbeque was still too dense for her. Stefan offered her half a steak from his overfull plate, but she declined with thanks. Markus came over and Marianne sat down with them, her baby on her arm.

'Well someone seems good and tired I reckon – how was your day, Lena?' Despite her weariness, Lena beamed.

'Fantastic!' She told Marianne all about her launches.

Just then, Maxl came by and put down a plate of sausages and potato salad with a bread roll in front of her.

'Thanks.' Lena looked up, surprised.

'Chef's orders – so you don't collapse over here. Maxl gave her a friendly pinch in the side and sat down with Bolle and another pilot two tables over. Piet nodded to her from the barbeque with a grin. Lena waved back.

'Gee, just because you're a girl! I don't see him looking after us,' grumbled Stefan.

'You should be happy! If he was looking after you, you wouldn't get a second helping,' said Markus with a playful sneer and a sidelong glance at Stefan's plate. Lena was content to enjoy her food and leave the others to their banter.

When it got dark, the boys lit a large campfire. Lena managed to keep up with the jokes for a while in the cosy firelight, but pretty soon her eyelids grew heavy and she crept off to her tent. In her sleeping bag, she remembered her new phone. She had wanted to give her mother a quick call... By the time she had decided it would have to wait till morning, she was already asleep.

The weather was kind to them. The next few days were also warm, and the thermals got going by late morning, right on cue. That meant plenty of cumulus clouds, the puffy white ones, for the cross-country pilots. For Lena and the other trainees it meant ideal training conditions. Even though Lena smeared herself with thick layers of sunscreen every day, by Wednesday night her nose was bright red. She wasn't alone though, everyone was somewhere from brown to red. The sun was just too strong. In the air, under the lens of the clear canopy, the effect was magnified.

Lena had a lot of launches and landings behind her and had collected quite a few hours of airtime. She had even completed her cable break exercises and spin training. The ASK21 crew had become a practiced team. The second two-seater wasn't used that much now. The advanced pupils had switched back to the single seaters after their aero-tow endorsements.

Maxl, Bolle and Marianne were off flying cross-country,

equipped with loggers. That meant they were flying a pre-determined course over land and the logger, a GPS device, permanently recorded all the data about where they flew. The logger prevented cheating. For example, without the logger, if you didn't find any thermals you could land at another airfield and take a launch again later. After the flight, the logger data would be analysed and evaluated.

Bolle flew a total of just on 80 kilometres. He would have liked to fly further, but when it got hard to find thermals he decided to fly back to the airfield. Marianne made it further. She had planned a 150-kilometre triangle in her LS4, but on the last leg after a total of 123 kilometres she didn't find any more thermals. While she still had some height, she searched for a suitable field to land in so as not to put herself in danger later at low altitude. Luckily she soon found a good spot with no trees or cows in the way where she could make a safe outlanding in the LS4.

The young trainees were fascinated, of course. Piet packed them all into his bus with the LS4 trailer hitched on behind. Fortunately they didn't have far to drive. Marianne had told them on the phone exactly where she and the LS4 were, so they found the field quite quickly.

The farmer who owned the land had watched the landing. He had brought the tractor and had already towed the glider close to the road with a rope. Marianne was very pleased to have such kind assistance. Some landowners were not in the least amused when a glider landed in their field. Especially if there was any damage to their crops or anything else of course. In this case there was no sign of the landing except a deep wheel rut where Marianne had landed.

Despite the warm weather over the last few days, the ground in this particular field was still very soft and wet. The help with the tractor was exactly what they needed. Pushing the glider by hand would have been hard work.

A few children and bystanders hung around and watched curiously as Piet, Marianne and the trainees started de-rigging the LS4 and stowing it in the trailer. Lena and Martin stood at one wing tip and tried to lift it as well as they could, to take the load off the main pins in the fuselage. Piet was trying to pull out the pins that held the wings and fuselage together.

'C'mon kids, put your backs into it, that's nowhere near enough' he spurred them on. Bolle, who was holding the other wing and sweating, complained.

'Oh great, and as soon as we've got this baby re-rigged, washed and back in the hangar, I suppose our cross country hero Maxl will call in and we'll have to head off again.'

'Nothing doing – we won't rig it till tomorrow,' puffed Piet, who had finally got the main pins out and was now easing the heavy end of the first wing out of its fuselage fittings. Once it was demounted, the wing was quite unwieldy. They carefully turned it up on edge and manoeuvred it into the custom fittings in the trailer.

'Man, that thing is heavy – you'd never believe it!' Martin rubbed his cramped fingers. Lena was soaked in sweat. She had panicked a little, thinking about how it would fall if her strength failed her.

'Did Piet tell you it's traditional for the pilot to treat the crew after an outlanding?' Marianne gasped, as she and Bolle struggled with the second wing.

'Perfect! A double banana split with cream and nuts,' said Stefan, with feeling. He was standing off to the side holding only the extracted main pins.

'Well *you've* really earned it haven't you?' Martin teased him.

'That's actually not a bad idea,' said Marianne. Lena didn't care – she just wanted a shower. They were all caked in dirt up to their knees, soaked in sweat and thirsty. It had already been a long day before they had set off. Lena had flown five launches in the morning and had a long thermal flight. With the heat, that had already been pretty much enough for her, and she was glad to join the retrieve crew for the change of scene. Really though, what a grind! Luckily it seemed that Marianne was either thinking along the same lines after her long flight...or she could read minds.

'Let's go back to the airfield first and pack everything away – then I'll shoot off again and bring back as much ice-cream as you can eat, OK?'

'You're an angel,' sighed Lena, feeling relieved, and flopped herself down in the grass. She left the other helpers to stow the tailplane and fuselage away.

'By the looks of you, I should wash you all down with the garden hose first off,' said Piet with a chuckle. Lena had actually landed more in the mud than the grass and was now completely filthy. Martin, who had been standing right beside her, had also been sprayed with mud and looked rather embarrassed. Stefan and Bolle howled with laughter at the disconcerted expressions on both of their faces. Seconds later they were pelted with wet lumps of earth. Of course they couldn't just let that pass...

'Marianne, do me a favour will you? If you have to land out, pick nice sunny fields and no more mud holes. Please!' Said Piet with a grin and a sidelong glance at the frantic battle in the churned up filth where the LS4 had sat a few moments before.

After they had stopped being silly, calmed down and brushed off the worst of the dirt, Piet took them all back to the airfield.

The others had also already packed up for the day. They simply left the LS4 in its trailer outside the hangar; they'd take care of it in the morning. Maxl came out to meet them.

'What happened to you lot?' He asked, looking at all the dirt. Everyone smirked, but nobody answered him.

'Well? Did you get round?' Bolle wanted to know. Maxl had set off on track almost at the same time as him, but had planned a much larger triangle, about 180 kilometres. Bolle was envious. Maxl only grinned.

'What do you reckon?' They both peeled off in the direction of the barbeque area, discussing the finer points of every individual thermal.

Lena grabbed her towel, fresh clothes, and a couple of titbits from her mother's basket and ambled off towards the showers. Martin and Stefan had disappeared with Piet. What were they up to this time? Twenty minutes later, her hair still wet, Lena was standing outside again clean and refreshed. The sky was slowly turning red. Apart from the murmuring of a few people around the barbeque, the airfield was wonderfully quiet and still. The tow plane had just landed and shut down the engine in front of the hangar.

'Look up there!' Maxl had come up behind her unnoticed and was pointing into the sunset. Lena didn't know what he meant at first, but then she found it. She recognized the silhouette of the ASK21 against the evening sky, quite high up.

'What are they doing up there? Spin training?' she asked Maxl.

'Something like that. Piet's taking advantage of the still air and doing some aerobatics. And today's winner is... Martin. He hassled Piet until he let him go along. Hopefully he doesn't repay him by spewing all over the cockpit,' replied Maxl.

Lena defended her friend.

'I doubt it, such a great pilot.' Martin had spent hours raving to her about aerobatics and describing individual manoeuvres in detail.

'If you say so, but aerobatics is another level again, not everyone can take it.' Maxl remained sceptical. The ASK21 was now directly over the airfield waggling its wings.

'That's to show he's starting his program,' explained Maxl. They leaned against the fence so as not to fall over, with their heads tilted right back. As the 21 put the nose down to build up speed for the first figure, Maxl suddenly pressed one of the earphones from his iPod into her hand. He had the other one in his own ear.

'Listen to this!'

Feeling a little stunned, Lena held the plug up to her ear.

An electric guitar solo built to a powerful crescendo at the exact moment that the 21 entered a loop. Lena got goosebumps and didn't move a muscle.

The music meshed with the glider movement as if it had been composed especially for it. Lena had never experienced anything like it.

The two-seater flew a languid roll and the melody flowed along with it at the same rate. As the 21 wheeled perfectly over the right wing in a stall turn, Lena could hear the notes literally spreading out, before the glider and the music joyously spun earthwards.

'That. Is. Beautiful.' whispered Lena fervently. She was completely rapt. Maxl took her hand and held it firmly.

Piet zoomed low over the runway at high speed one more time, made a steep turn and came in for landing fully unruffled.

'He's got what it takes. That was crazy!' enthused Maxl. Lena swallowed and handed him the earpiece.

'Thanks.' She didn't dare look him in the eyes. Instead she

quietly sighed 'I want to be able to fly like that one day.'

'Why not? Of course you will.' Only now did Maxl let go of her hand again. He grinned a satisfied grin and flitted off to help Piet and Martin push the glider back. Lena watched him go in a daze, then she ran after him.

11. Kim Arrives

'Did you see that beat up? Fwoar! We had 230 klicks on the clock and then he just pulled up, turned the glider around and there we were, set up on final as if it was a measly circuit… and in the roll – you can't imagine – when you just hang there inverted – totally wicked!' Martin had red ears and shining eyes. He continued trying to put his elation into words. Lena was still somewhat agitated herself – and it certainly wasn't to do with the aerobatics display. She understood where Martin was coming from though.

Maxl rolled his eyes and whispered to Lena, 'Look out, this may take some time. Hopefully he won't completely snap.' Lena didn't say anything. She wasn't sure that she wouldn't lift off just like Martin. What about Maxl anyway? Wasn't he the same about his own flights? They all pushed the two-seater back to the hangar, washed the insects off the leading edges, and put away the battery and parachutes.

In the meantime, Marianne had returned with mountains of ice cream and they had to hurry, otherwise Bolle and Stefan would have demolished the lion's share and left the rest to melt. They all sat around the campfire until late into the night again.

Lena called her mother now and then with reports on proceedings. Barbara was overwhelmed by the things her daughter was telling her. It was still hard for her to come to terms with her little girl belting across the airfield in the launch point bus, much less flying a plane.

She never had understood aeronautical details particularly well anyway and she had no chance at all of remembering all the new names.

'Lena, you'll have to show me all that again in person, you know. I'm trying to keep everything in my head but it's all too much. Oh yeah and we'll be there tomorrow with Kim. She's not coming by train after all. Her mother still has some appointment or other around here and wants to bring Kim herself. Isn't that great?' she interrupted Lena's rave.

'Oh yeah, that's great,' replied Lena listlessly. On the one hand she had been missing Kim for such a long time and wanted to show her everything there was to show. On the other, she also had a slightly depressing feeling that her friend might not be quite so overjoyed with life on the airfield as she was. She said goodbye to her mother with mixed feelings and walked back to the campfire, deep in thought.

The next morning was significantly cooler. They didn't expect much in the way of thermals, so Fritz had them practicing quick circuits off the winch. Take-off, land, up, down, push the glider... For Lena, Markus and Stefan it was a lot of running. Simple circuits like that took scarcely three minutes.

Things were a lot quieter for the other pilots; most of the gliders were still in the hangar. After Fritz had flown six circuits with each of his charges and declared that one more would make him giddy, they decided to take an extended lunch break.

They pushed the ASK21 off to the side and put a tyre on one wing tip, so the glider wouldn't fly solo in a strong gust. There was coffee and leisurely chat at the launch point. Marianne, Maxl and Bolle planned their upcoming cross-country flights.

A few people presented their logbooks to the relevant instructors. Every single launch had to be recorded in the logbook.

The instructors made notes about each trainee's latest advances in their training progress sheets.

Martin tried to persuade Piet to do some more aerobatics.

'You should learn to fly straight and level consistently first, my boy,' smirked Piet. 'Anyway, cloud base isn't high enough today. We don't do aerobatics that low.'

'Lena, you've got visitors.' Bolle pointed to the camping area. Barbara was standing there, waving in their direction. Kim was standing next to her, looking a little lost. Lena trotted off. Her little brother Jakob raced out to meet her.

'Hello. – Jakob, you can't just run straight across the runway like that! You have to look first and make sure no planes are coming in,' she scolded him good-naturedly.

'But you just ran over here too,' Jakob defended himself.

'True, but in the first place *I* looked, and in the second I already knew there was nothing in the air at the moment. – Kim!' The two friends fell into each other's arms. 'I've missed you so much.' Lena hugged Kim hard. All her doubts had vanished. Even if Kim didn't want to fly – they would understand each other.

'Finally!' Kim looked around curiously. 'Not much going on here is there? I thought there'd be heaps of people and gliders …?'

'Oh, you'll see them soon enough. The weather's boring today and we've all flown so much in the last few days, that's why we're chilling out a bit now. I've flown six flights today.'

'On your own? Hello darling.' Barbara embraced Lena, looking aghast.

'No, with Fritz,' laughed Lena.

'Who's this Fritz?' Kim wanted to know. 'Didn't you say you'd been flying with a Piet?'

'He's another instructor, I'll tell you everything, come on!

Bring all your stuff to my tent first!' Lena took Kim to the camping area.

'But I want to go to the planes,' whined Jakob. He had to be patient for a while in spite of himself though. They put Kim's things in Lena's tent and then Lena showed Kim the clubhouse, the hangar and everything else she needed to make herself at home.

The girls babbled away incessantly along the way. Barbara and Jakob strung along behind them and listened intently, especially to Lena's airfield adventures.

Eventually they got to the launch point. Barbara was glad of the coffee that Marianne held out to her while Lena excitedly introduced her friend to everyone. Kim received an enthusiastic welcome, which obviously pleased her enormously, but she still couldn't be persuaded to try even a circuit with Piet in the 21.

'Well then – no cross-country training without a good retrieve crew. Are you spoken for?' asked Bolle, pragmatically.

'Can I? Can I? Then I can fly right? Mami, can I?' Jakob saw that his chance had come. Barbara looked at Piet questioningly.

'If Piet can take you?'

Piet grinned.

'All right then young man, let's go! You take the wingtip and steer the two-seater back to the launch point while we push.' Jakob immediately jumped to it excitedly.

'Uh-oh,' Lena wouldn't have put it past her brother to accidentally steer a wing into the launch point bus. She sprinted after him. Kim smiled uncertainly. She couldn't quite determine whether retrieve crew was something desirable or not. Marianne took Barbara and Kim under her wing and they followed Lena, Jakob, Piet and a couple of boys who were helping push the 21 to the launch point. Barbara watched proudly as Lena put the parachute on her brother and helped him climb into the cockpit as a matter of course. She explained the instruments to him and told him where to hold on – just like Martin had done with her not so very long ago.

Jakob was glowing with excitement and at the same time he was trying to look cool and not let it show too much. Of course Barbara saw through him, much to her private amusement. Then they all had to stand back and Lena hooked on the cable.

'What an effort,' mumbled Kim to herself. As soon as the glider was in the air, Lena set off down the runway to be ready to push back after the landing. She took Kim with her.

'Hop to it! They'll be back down in a moment! There's no thermals in this weather, they can't get away.'

'Is this how it goes the whole time? Run, push, up, down?' Kim pulled a not so enthusiastic expression.

'Pretty much, yeah… when we're training… of course in good weather the gliders are away for much longer. But you do get to fly yourself,' said Lena, trying somewhat cautiously to justify herself.

'Well if *that* makes all that hassle worthwhile for you, then I can put up with it for a couple of days,' grinned Kim. 'But don't think you're getting me in one of those contraptions. What did that guy mean by *retrieve crew* by the way? What's his name again? He was sweet!'

Oh that's all right then, thought Lena with relief, she may not want to fly, but as long as there are enough boys to flirt with everything seems to be fine.

After the landing, Jakob was torn between two feelings: total excitement that he had got to fly, and disappointment that the flight had been so short.

Bolle and Martin consoled him with a promise that he could help retrieve the cables in a moment.

'Oh, oh, can I drive?' asked Jakob.

'Are you tall enough to see over the wheel?' grinned Bolle. The boys drafted Jakob and Kim into the ground operation, much to the satisfaction of both. Barbara chatted to Marianne and Piet at the launch point. Lena, Markus and Stefan went back to their circuits and Fritz kept them working and sweating.

It was already evening when Barbara said her goodbyes and dragged a protesting Jakob off towards the car.

'We'll be back in a couple of days anyway to pick the girls up. I'm sure you can help again then. Bye, Lena, see you on Sunday night.'

Later, when everything was packed away and the ASK21 was washed and in the hangar, Lena and Kim finally had time to catch up in peace. Naturally there were plenty of topics they didn't want to discuss with curious mothers or brothers hanging around. As the boys sat down around the campfire again, the two girls were still huddled together outside Lena's tent. Lena gave Kim all the minutiae of everything that had happened in the last week. Admittedly Kim wasn't all that interested in the flying side of things, but to make up for that she was all the more enthralled with everything that had anything to do with Maxl, Bolle and the other boys.

'Wow, goosebumps,' sighed Kim, spellbound. 'He just took your hand, just like that, and then the music and the aerobatics… in the sunset. He's a bit of a romantic, isn't he? Nothing like that ever happens to me. Did he say anything else after that?'

'No, that's just it,' rejoined Lena, 'I really don't know what to think. After Martin's landing he ran off as if nothing had even happened or like it was just totally normal.'

'Do you think he could be shy?' asked Kim.

'Oh no, I'm pretty sure about that,' Lena laughed. 'Lack of self confidence is definitely not one of his problems, just ask Bolle.'

'Oh yeah, I will,' grinned Kim. 'You can be sure of that! And what about Martin?' She probed.

'Why Martin?' Lena wondered. 'What about him?'

'Well hello! – You're always so naive! He already worshipped you before, and now you're suddenly his best gliding buddy too and you expect him to just be cool with that? No way!' smirked Kim.

Lena shook her head emphatically.

'You're crazy, there's nothing there.'

Kim raised her hands in a conciliatory gesture.

'It's all good, no worries – maybe I only imagined it before? So tell me – has Philipp been here too? I mean, seeing as how Martin's his best friend and all?' Kim looked at Lena expectantly. 'He wrote something or other: see you around, or something like that – maybe he'll drop in over the weekend?'

Lena was sceptical.

'Well, he hasn't been here yet, and thinking about how he always makes fun of us so much, I can't imagine it. Isabella's totally got him wrapped around her little finger too – I'm pretty sure he's not going to let himself be seen around here anytime soon.'

'Oh well, his loss,' breathed Kim disappointedly. 'Come on, let's go to the campfire – if that's how he wants it, he can stay stolen.'

12. Aborted Take-off

The next morning they started early as usual. Briefing was at eight o'clock. Lena shook Kim to wake her up.

'Come on! Get up! Breakfast! Briefing!'

'Whaddlllidothere…,' muttered Kim, pulling her sleeping bag up over her head. 'I can come later. Itsholidaysisnit.' Then she just went back to sleep. Lena thought about it for a moment and let her friend sleep on. If she's not interested in flying… she thought to herself.

Lena was actually pretty tired herself, but the sun was already shining very promisingly – it was going to be a wonderful day. They wouldn't have to grind out circuits. Thermalling was on the menu.

The night before had gone on endlessly again. Despite the many flying stories and plans the boys had made for today, Kim had not felt left out. It was fun and relaxed and in the end it was very late before the fire had burned right down. Lena did envy Kim a little, that she could simply turn over and go back to sleep.

She slipped into her jeans and pulled a sweatshirt over her head, then she crawled out of the tiny tent being careful not to disturb Kim any further. At the breakfast buffet in the clubhouse she grabbed a croissant and a pot of coffee.

'Am I glad I don't have my driving licence yet, or I'd have to go and get bread rolls in the mornings too.'

She let herself drop onto the bench by the window with a contented sigh. Martin was sitting next to her.

'What's the forecast this morning?' she asked, tucking into her breakfast. Maxl came around the corner with Bolle in tow.

'This is weather for creating legends,' he announced, beaming.

'I thought you wanted to fly a 300K triangle today?' retorted Martin drily. 'Cloud base up to 1200 metres, visibility from sea to sea. Ha! Should be child's play.' Maxl completely ignored him.

'Show off,' Bolle reproached him.

'Really? You're going to try for 300 kilometres today?' Lena swallowed. 'Have you ever declared a triangle that big before?'

'Have no fear Princess, I'll get around in nothing flat and be there to catch your wing on the last landing of the day,' declared Maxl cockily.

'Show-off,' grumbled Bolle again.

'What are you planning?' Martin wanted to know from Bolle. '150 kilometres?'

'We don't all have to have delusions of grandeur like Monsieur,' Bolle nodded, with a sideways glance at Maxl.

Maxl grinned.

'I want to try for my five hour duration flight today,' announced Martin proudly.

'Have fun with that. Five hours circling over the airfield… I remember it well, a real drudge. They won't let you go cross-country before you've done it though; Piet is really strict about it. Make sure you have a good pee first! I tell you, I nearly burst by the end,' Maxl advised him.

'Can I have everyone's attention please!' Piet started the briefing. The weather forecast was just as good as Maxl had claimed. As always, Piet spelled out who should fly what, where, with whom and when.

Then everyone charged out to get the planes out of the hangar.

Lena, Markus and Stefan had the ASK21 to themselves again.

'Now, you fledglings,' announced Fritz a little later when the gliders where all checked and everything was set up at the launch point, 'after lunch I'll be taking some naps. This morning you can fly three more circuits each as a warm up. In the afternoon the thermals will have got going and you can each have a long flight, about an hour, and I'll pretend I'm not even on board. I won't help with thermalling or any decisions. You can thermal in the circuit area. After an hour, come back down and manage the sink so that it works out. If you bomb out earlier, break off in time to fly to the circuit joining area and arrive with enough height to join downwind in the normal way. I don't want to be practicing outlandings in the circuit area with any of you. Is that clear? Stefan goes first!'

That sounded like hard work, but Lena was determined to do her very best. She really wanted to stay up in a thermal alone and manage the circuit and landing herself without Fritz having to take over or say anything. The other two seemed to have similar feelings. All three of them were raring to go. There wouldn't be any aerotows today; they hadn't taken the Cessna out of the hangar. Piet thought the weather would be good enough that everyone could find a thermal from a winch launch.

There was no sign of Kim. Now and then Lena wondered how Kim could possibly still be asleep with all the bustle around the airfield. Wild horses couldn't have kept Lena in the tent any longer with everything that was going on. Then she was too busy and completely forgot about Kim.

Before long, they had all flown their three circuits. The thermals were bubbling away nicely and after a short break Stefan would be getting ready for the first of the long flights, or *Fritz's naps.*

Markus and Stefan boasted to each other about which of them had the better nose for thermals.

'When two fight the third wins,' teased Lena with a grin.

'If God had wanted women to fly, he would have made the sky pink,' countered Stefan.

'Oh no! Not that old chestnut,' Maxl defended her on the way past to his glider. 'I don't believe it. Won't those moronic sayings ever die out?'

'You won't see her for dust, boys.' Fritz gave Stefan a more or less friendly rap on the head with his knuckle and then ran after Maxl to give him a few last minute tips for his 300. Maxl didn't actually have his gliding licence; he wasn't 16 yet. He still had to fly under direct supervision from an instructor.

Lena poked her tongue out at Stefan with a grin.

'The winner buys the next round of ice cream. I can be generous.'

'Agreed, but don't you sound confident! Look, Kim's awake,' Markus pointed to the camping area. Kim gave a quick wave and disappeared, headed for the showers. Maxl was flying the LS4 today. Lena helped him strap in and hooked on the cable.

'Good luck! I hope you get around OK. I'll keep my fingers crossed!' She called out to him at the last moment before lifting the wing for the launch.

'You too, keep your chin up! You can do it. I'll be thinking of you,' replied Maxl, but she could hardly hear him; the glider was already rolling. Lena ran to keep up and eventually let go of the wing when the LS4 got too fast for her. Oh yes! She didn't want to disappoint Maxl! She paid careful attention to where he found the first thermal after the launch. She might find something there herself later. Stefan was next to launch. Apparently he had also paid attention to where Maxl had flown. He flew in the same direction and seemed to connect with the bubble. Lena and Markus followed his circles in the sky as if mesmerised.

Suddenly they heard yelling at the launch point.

'Stop, stop, stop!' Marianne shouted down the telephone to the winch driver. Several people waved agitatedly and called out, 'Stop there!' Then Lena spotted Kim! She was running merrily towards them and didn't seem to notice that she would run directly into the path of the K8 that was already hooked onto the next cable.

'Kim! Go back!' Lena was shouting now too. The K8, with Martin on board, nudged forward a little and the cable stayed tight. Kim pulled up in shock, but not far enough away. There was a sharp bang and the cable shot out of the glider release and raced away towards the winch. Martin had reacted lightning fast and released. He pulled air brakes, trying to bleed off the momentum as much as possible. Fortunately the K8 had not yet built up much speed and he was able to stop after a few metres. Kim was still standing on the same spot, stock still from shock and staring wide-eyed at Martin in his glider. Martin was no less shocked. His hands trembled a little as he opened the K8 canopy. Kim gradually came out of her stupor and went over to him with wobbly knees. There was no holding back now. Everyone jumped up and crowded around the K8.

'I'm so sorry,' Kim burst out, 'Lena did explain everything to me, but I mustn't have been paying attention, I don't know, I completely forgot.' Kim had tears in her eyes.

'Kim! Are you OK? Didn't you see the glider?' Lena ran over and embraced her friend. Kim was white as a sheet.

'You reacted fast.' Bolle clapped Martin approvingly on the shoulder as he climbed out of the cockpit.

Everyone talked over each other loudly.

'Calm down! No harm done,' Piet's voice rang out over the startled mob.

'Well done,' he praised Martin. 'Everything OK, young lady? That won't happen to you again, that's for sure. Reminds us all how important it is to always look out wherever we go. Eyes open on the airfield! Now I think we could all do with a break and a coffee.' He led Kim and Martin over to the launch point reassuringly. The others pushed the K8 back again and then followed them. Marianne distributed coffee and biscuits. Bolle drove off to retrieve the cables. After a while they had all calmed down again. Martin disappeared briefly to the toilet. He still wanted to launch on his five-hour flight anyway.

'Shouldn't Stefan be landing soon by the way?' asked Lena. 'The hour's nearly up isn't it?'

'Bombed out, bombed out,' crowed Markus.

'No,' Lena contradicted him, 'they're coming.' She had found the ASK21 in the sky. 'Kim, are you staying here at the table or will you come and push?' asked Lena, feeling concerned for her friend.

'I think I'll stay here for a while, thanks.' Kim wasn't planning on going anywhere in a hurry. She could still feel the shock in her arms and legs. Lena and Markus trotted off to get the 21.

'The bar is set pretty high kids; Stefan did very well. Are you ready now Lena?' Fritz was in a good mood after the landing

'Nothing to it – terrific thermals,' Stefan trumpeted with a smirk, 'your turn, hot-shot.'

'Idiot,' grumbled Lena to herself. She ardently hoped she would find enough lift too.

13. Lena Looks for Thermals

No sooner had Lena released the cable than she felt her left wing lifting.

'Cool,' she rejoiced, 'that thermal is mine.' Fritz deliberately said nothing at all and relaxed back into his seat.

Lena moved the stick and rudder to the left, commencing the left turn. Centralise the controls, just a bit of up elevator to hold the nose on the horizon. To her satisfaction the variometer showed a good two metres per second climb. She was well centred in the thermal and hardly had to make any corrections. In no time they had spiralled up to 850 metres. Then the thermal died out and Lena had to try her luck elsewhere.

In the process she lost some of her height. She gradually grew more anxious again. She hadn't even been in the air for 20 minutes yet. She didn't want to bomb out now. She flew to the spot where Maxl and Stefan had found lift earlier, but there was nothing there now. Lena gnashed her teeth. What rotten luck!

She was too low to fly far from the airfield to search for other thermals. Two more circles at the most and she'd have to fly to the circuit joining area and join downwind. Her fervent prayer went unanswered; she couldn't find any more lift. Lena decided to land…

'Before I really stuff it up and we have to outland,' she deliberated out loud, assessing her options. Not a peep from Fritz. All at once Lena found herself in a bad mood. Couldn't he even give a tiny hint about where a thermal might be found, she thought angrily.

Stefan was sure to be laughing up his sleeve and big noting himself right now!

She turned onto base and then onto final, deploying the airbrakes. First half airbrake and then, as the aiming point continued to sink in her field of view, full brakes. Just before the aiming point, her gaze shifted back to the horizon. She eased back on the stick and flew the last few metres parallel to the ground before gently touching down and rolling to a stop. The ASK21 hesitated for a moment and then gradually tipped to the left, coming to rest with the left wing tip on the ground.

'Oh great,' she moaned, as she saw Stefan and Markus coming over with smirks on their faces, 'here we go.' As she opened the canopy, Fritz finally opened his mouth.

'Lena, that was far and away your best landing yet. Well done. And you had the courage to make an unpleasant decision in good time without my help. I'm impressed. Don't give yourself a hard time just because there were no thermals there – that happens to the best pilots. You did exactly the right thing. Safety first. Perfect!'

Only now did Lena realise that she had just landed the glider without any input whatsoever from Fritz. She had been so distracted by her own annoyance about the thermals that she actually hadn't missed the running commentary. Stefan had been about to launch into one of his caustic sayings, but his mouth suddenly clapped shut again.

'Didn't Fritz say anything while you were landing? Did you do everything yourself?' he demanded to know as they were pushing back. Lena skipped jauntily along at the wingtip.

'Yep! And I didn't even think about it, just happened automatically,' she couldn't refrain from adding.

Now she was quite pleased with herself again.

Markus had better luck. Like Stefan he was able to stay up for almost an hour. In the meantime, Lena had had time enough to take care of Kim, who had now recovered from her shock.

To top it all off, Lena took another launch in the afternoon. This time she easily managed her longer flight. Without knowing it, Martin was a great help in the K8. Lena simply followed him as he tirelessly circled around near the airfield in pursuit of his five hours. Of course she had to be careful to leave enough clearance and turn in the same direction as him in the thermals.

'Now you're making it easy for yourself,' chuckled Fritz, 'Look! Martin's waving to you.' Lena waved back. If only she could really fly on her own too. In the end they landed one after the other, Lena first.

'Are the five hours up already?' she called to him after climbing out of the cockpit. Without answering, Martin hobbled off hurriedly towards the trees with cramped steps.

'That wasn't five hours,' remarked Fritz dryly, 'that was a weak bladder.'

Bolle was already back too, and quite satisfied with his flight. Only Maxl was still out. It would soon be evening, and they gradually started to pack up.

'I can't believe it – four hours twenty minutes. So close. But I just couldn't hold out any longer,' Martin lamented.

Suddenly a loud whistling noise whooshed over them and away.

'That'll be Maxl,' called Bolle. Sure enough, the LS4 shot low over the airfield, diagonally across the runway, pulled up on the other side and came in for a perfectly elegant landing.

'Young hoon,' Piet grinned, but he was shaking his head as well. Yet again Bolle grumbled something that sounded like:

'WhaddidIsay – such a show-off…' He let it go at that though. Perhaps he was in a good mood. Kim had been excessively adoring since he landed.

As always it was another boisterous evening around the campfire and everyone's achievements were thoroughly celebrated. Besides, the weather prognosis for the next few days wasn't at all good. That meant they would probably pack up their tents the next day and that would be the end of the gliding camp. Lena savoured the evening to the full. Everyone joked and talked over each other in a jumble. Kim, too, seemed to be thoroughly enjoying herself. She sat between Bolle and Maxl, quietly listening to their stories.

Maxl enthusiastically related the details of his flight. How he was all but forced to outland a hundred kilometres away. How, at the last moment, he could make out a falcon climbing in a thermal off a ridge. How Maxl had valiantly tried his luck there too.

'For ten minutes or more I just followed that bird. It was amazing; the falcon didn't care at all. One time it came really close. I was worried it might feel threatened and attack, but pretty soon after that it disappeared.'

Martin was somewhat humbled after breaking off his five-hour flight early. On the other hand he basked in the praise of his quick reactions when Kim had run in front of the glider.

Piet sat down with Lena.

'So, what do you think, are you in? Should I talk to your parents tomorrow and sort out your club membership? The gliding camp was a huge success for you. You're doing really well, a couple of weekends of good weather and you'll be flying solo.'

'Absolutely,' Lena beamed enthusiastically. 'I already arranged everything with my mother on the phone a little while ago. They'll all be coming to pick us up tomorrow.' Lena glowed with pride over the praise. She couldn't wait to earn her wings!

The last of the logs were soon burned away and it got distinctly cooler. One after the other, nearly everyone went to bed. Apart from Lena and Kim, only Piet, two other older pilots, Bolle and Martin were still sitting around the fire pit.

Maxl had just disappeared around the corner. He reappeared suddenly, driving the Lepo, and waved them over.

'Come with me!' Lena and Kim gave each other a questioning look. Martin and Bolle had already run over with a whoop. The girls shrugged their shoulders and trotted along after them.

'Don't go causing me any trouble, OK?' Piet called after them before turning his attention back to his beer. He didn't seem particularly concerned.

Giggling, Lena and Kim squeezed themselves into the back seat with Martin, between the toolbox and a tail dolly.

'What are we doing?' Lena wanted to know.

'It's a surprise,' replied Maxl secretively. They drove through the darkness to the other end of the airfield. Maxl stopped the car next to the threshold of the 09 asphalt runway and turned off the engine and the lights. It was now pitch dark. Out here there were no lanterns, no lights, nothing. They fumbled their way out of the car. Maxl was already on the runway tinkering with something or other. Suddenly they heard music.

'We are the champions…' boomed out into the night.

'Not you and your golden oldies again,' whined Bolle.

'Shut up Bolle. Then bring something yourself, dude!' Maxl kept his cool. 'Come over here and sit down everyone, the asphalt is still really warm,' he invited them.

In the meantime, their eyes had got used to the darkness. A couple of stars twinkled from between the clouds. Maxl lay stretched out full length on the asphalt staring into the sky. He had his iPod beside him with two speakers. The girls tentatively moved closer. Kim laughed nervously.

'Isn't that much too loud?' asked Lena apprehensively.

'Ah nuts, who's going to hear it out here? Come here Princess, there's room for you here on my right…' Maxl reassured her. Lena sat down next to him. The other two boys were already lying down too.

'Cool,' Martin called out. Lena felt the warm asphalt with her hand.

'It really is warm – and it wasn't even such a warm day,' she said, astounded.

Kim had stretched herself out between Maxl and Bolle and was whispering something to Bolle. Lena slid over a bit and lay back too. Seen from above they must now form a star shape, she thought. They lay in a circle with their heads in the middle, soaked up the warmth of the runway, listened to the music, and gazed up at the stars between the wisps of cloud. For a while no one said anything, then they all started talking at once. Maxl offered up his story of the falcon again, only this time he stood up in the dark and demonstrated the flight manoeuvres. He tripped over their legs and fell back into the middle laughing. The girls shrieked.

Martin grumbled, 'Watch out won't you! My hand only just got better again.'

'Sorry, sorry, sorry,' laughed Maxl jovially. Bolle was reminded of some episode from an old class excursion and he fell into relating a long epic, with active encouragement from Maxl. The two of them were having a great time. Kim giggled incessantly. Lena looked around surreptitiously to see if that was purely prompted by the story or if there was something else going on behind their backs. She couldn't make out anything in the darkness though.

Maxl was lying on Lena's left again and had propped himself up on his elbows. Casually, almost incidentally, his fingers started playing with Lena's hair and gently stroking her head. She could feel her heart beating. Maxl and Bolle continued with their narration. Suddenly something nudged her hand on the other side.

Oh, please no, thought Lena. That was Martin! Was Kim right after all? Lena pulled her hand away. Maybe it was accidental? She hadn't deceived herself though; after a while she noticed Martin's hand cautiously seeking her out again. That was too much. Lena sprang up.

'OK, ah, sorry everyone, but ...don't you think it's getting too cold? I'm probably just too tired,' she stammered awkwardly. Maxl stretched and yawned.

'You're right – should we go back?'

Kim shot Lena a questioning look, but Lena had already retreated to the Lepo and disappeared into the passenger seat. Maxl packed up his stuff and the others clambered into the back seat. Bolle kept up his story. Kim had daringly slipped her arm through Bolle's and was leaning her head on his shoulder. Maxl bombed across the airfield, foot flat to the floor, towards the camping area, where everything was now peaceful.

At first Martin was very quiet and Lena felt quite apprehensive. Then he got his foot stuck in the toolbox and started swearing. That was so typically slapstick that everyone had to laugh. Lena turned around briefly as she laughed, and they looked each other in the eyes for a moment. Totally normal. What was I worrying about? Such rubbish, Lena thought to herself with relief. Kim had me all worked up.

Maxl parked the Lepo in front of the hangar and they all quickly scampered to their tents before Piet could get upset about the noise of the car.

14. Huge Disappointment

The next morning, sure enough, everything was grey on grey and raining. It was still very quiet in the caravans and everyone slept in. Barbara, Johannes and Jakob arrived early to pick up the girls. Kim packed up the tent with Johannes and Jakob while Barbara and Lena went through the paperwork with Piet.

'All good my dear,' said Piet, delighted. 'See you next weekend here at the airfield. Come if you can, even if the weather's no good. There's a lot of theory to learn and plenty of work to do around the place. I'll look forward to seeing you.'

After heartfelt goodbyes to Piet they helped Kim and the boys pack up. Martin had crawled out of his tent too and started dismantling it.

'This is much easier,' he was pleased to discover.

'Question is whether you'll ever be able to put it up again, the way you're tearing at it,' sneered Bolle. He and Maxl were just finishing their breakfast. Maxl got up.

'I can't watch! Come on I'll give you a hand. Lena, did you sign up?'

'Yep, I'm in,' said Lena happily.

'Well then, welcome to the family,' said Maxl, and planted a loud kiss on her cheek on his way past. Kim stared wide-eyed and Lena blushed.

'Ah, yeah, thanks,' she stammered.

'Till next weekend at the latest then, or maybe see you at school.'

'Yeah, cool, till then.'

'Lena, I'll be in touch later about the movies, I'll give you a call,' came Martin's muffled voice from under the groundsheet. Kim gave Lena an I-told-you-so grin. Lena had described the grotesque scene on the runway last night to Kim more than once.

'Maxl on the one side and then Martin as well! What's wrong with him?' Lena had said, feeling really annoyed. Kim had very wisely made no comment.

Everybody was laughing.

'Yep, good. Ciao everybody.' Lena got into the car. In the light of day, Bolle obviously wasn't so sure whether he should hug Kim or not, and he just patted her awkwardly on the back as they parted.

'See you round.'

The girls waved, and they set off for home. It turned into a quiet, pleasant day.

In the afternoon, Paul came around and they had to give a blow-by-blow account of their time on the airfield. Paul regarded his daughter with some satisfaction. She was suntanned and had a glint in her eye and was proudly relating her adventures. Kim cut in constantly with extra details.

'So, you really enjoyed yourselves,' Paul was pleased. 'I guess we'll be spending our weekends on the airfield in future, right? I hope it won't be too much with your schoolwork.'

'It doesn't have to be every weekend,' Barbara chimed in. The girls weren't really listening though.

'Are you going to take up flying too, Kim?' Paul asked.

'No, it's not my thing, but I'll come along to the airfield when I visit Lena – that was great fun.'

Martin rang in the evening and they all arranged to go to the cinema the next afternoon.

'Philipp and Isabella are coming too,' Lena warned Kim, feeling concerned.

'Hm. You know what?' Kim flopped onto her bed in Lena's room with a reflective look at her friend, 'I don't mind at all! I'm OK with it. I don't know what I ever saw in him.'

'Are you sure? In that case…' Lena was relieved. She thought she knew where this change of heart sprang from.

'Shame Bolle's grandparents are visiting this weekend,' Kim promptly sighed.

'How do you know that?' asked Lena.

'He just texted me – I asked him if he wants to come to the movies,' explained Kim. Lena grinned.

'Then I really don't have to worry about you, do I?'

'What about Maxl?' Kim held her phone out to Lena.

'Why? No. I don't even know his number,' Lena parried uncertainly.

'But you'd want to, wouldn't you?' Kim probed persistently. Lena squirmed a little.

'Yeah, kinda…' she admitted.

'He has been more than attentive to you,' said Kim in a matter-of-fact way. 'I think he seriously likes you.' Lena turned red.

'Do you really think so? Maybe he's just, you know, always like that?'

'You'll find out soon enough, there'll be plenty more weekends – and you'll see him at school in the breaks too!' Kim raised her eyebrows suggestively. Jakob came noisily into the room and they didn't explore the subject in any further depth. For the rest of the evening they lazed around watching DVDs.

The next morning at eight o'clock, Lena rolled over in bed again contentedly. She could hear her brother noisily storming through the house. Finally getting to sleep in! Kim was still fast asleep. It would be a late breakfast.

Afterwards they sat at the computer for ages and for once Barbara didn't say anything. Holidays and bad weather…

Johannes dropped the girls off outside the cinema at four o'clock. They had agreed to meet half an hour later, but they wanted to go to the café next door first. It was full, and busy.

'Wow! Half the school must be here,' Kim was clearly delighted. They found a free table and quickly ordered. Kim was soon surrounded by several old classmates asking questions about Berlin. She didn't seem to mind the attention at all. Lena smiled to herself. Their milkshakes arrived just as Isabella and Philipp appeared, with Martin in tow, and came over to them.

'Hiiii, we thought we'd find you here. Long time no see, Kim, how's it going?' Isabella pushed through the crowd, hugged Kim, and to Lena's astonishment acted exceedingly amicably. Philipp on the other hand was being rather reserved and seemed vaguely annoyed.

'Hi, Kim. Lena – wow, aren't you brown? What happened?' Martin cuffed him in the side.

'Airfield,' he reminded him.

'Of course. I forgot all about that. How was it?' Philipp asked curiously. Lena wondered what was up with him – so friendly all of a sudden. She had expected him to find new ways to needle her about it. They're both behaving pretty strangely today, she thought. Lena was about to answer him when her eyes happened to wander to the door and she saw… Maxl!

Not only Maxl; he had his arm around a tall, slender girl with long, glossy, dark hair. He said something to the girl.

She turned and gave him a long kiss. They both laughed.

Then they kissed again.

'Earth to Lena – hello! Anyone home?' Philipp waved his hand in front of her eyes. 'It can't have been that bad, can it?'

'What? No, it was great.' Lena tore her eyes away from the prospect of the couple in the entrance and shook her head vacantly.

'I'll be right back.' She grabbed her jacket and made a beeline for the toilets.

'What's up with her? Did I say something wrong?' Philipp watched her go, taken aback.

Isabella interrupted her discussion with Kim.

'Can we go now? The show'll start any moment.'

Martin pointed in the direction Lena had just disappeared in.

'Fine by me – but Lena isn't back yet – Kim, maybe you could see what's keeping her?' Kim glanced up. She hadn't even noticed Lena's absence until now.

'She'll be done in a moment for sure – let's wait outside.' She quickly paid for them both. On the way out she passed Maxl and the girl. Maxl greeted Martin and Kim with a wry grin. Kim stared wide-eyed.

'I think I'll just check up on Lena after all. Go on in, we'll be along soon.' Then she was gone.

'Well, I don't know what you do with the girls on the airfield, but they seem rather unsettled today, don't they?' Philipp wondered. Martin shrugged.

'No idea – they'll be out soon enough.'

Isabella hurried them both along towards the cinema.

Lena held on tight to the basin and stared into the mirror, dumbfounded. Kim came in and took her in her arms without a word. The corners of Lena's mouth quivered. She pressed her lips together. She didn't want to admit that a whole little world had just collapsed for her. She certainly didn't want to walk right through the café with teary eyes, past everybody.

'There's always ads at the start. We'll wait a moment. They might leave.' Kim didn't need words to understand her.

'But if we go out in ten minutes and they're still there it'll be pretty embarrassing…' Lena murmured, sounding tormented.

'OK, if it comes to that I'll go out first and distract them,' Kim decided.

She tentatively led Lena to the door and along the passage to the café. Maxl and his girlfriend were nowhere to be seen. Relieved, the girls went outside.

'Do you still feel like seeing the movie?' asked Kim.

'No, but I'm sure you do, don't you? It's been so long since you saw everybody,' sniffled Lena.

'Forget it, it's not so important! Tomorrow morning they'll already have forgotten I was even here. And I really could do without listening to Isabella's smarminess…She must have found out about my emails with Philipp. But what do I care?' Kim linked arms with Lena.

Lena sniffed, 'Do you think I'm stupid? I mean, I could have asked him if he had a girlfriend, I didn't even consider it. He was always just so nice and totally attentive.'

'I know. I thought so too. Why didn't she ever come to the airfield?' Kim reassured her friend, 'and YOU aren't stupid at all. I never want to hear that again! I'll send Martin a quick text. I'll say you're not feeling well and we're going home. It's true after all. He doesn't need to know *why* it's true.'

Lena and Kim took the bus home. Barbara and Johannes weren't there. They had been invited for dinner with friends and were already on the way. Jakob was staying over with Grandma

Liesl. Kim went to ransack the pantry and returned to Lena's room carrying ice cream, gummy bears, chips and two small bottles of Barbara's homemade herb lemonade. Lena's mother was particularly proud of this recipe and only presented the brew on special occasions.

'So, I hope I don't get in trouble with your mother – but this is an emergency,' she declared, 'aaannd: music!' She bent over to scoop up the remote for the stereo. It was the last straw. Her arms were still full and one of the bottles slipped out of her hand. They both dived to save it and their heads came together in a direct, full-on crash.

'Ouch!'

'Uugh!'

The bottle fell to the floor and broke with a pathetic tinkle. The lemonade foamed out on the carpet. For a moment Lena and Kim looked at each other in shock, then they both snorted with laughter.

'Oh, how awful! Thanks, that was just what I needed! Haha! I'm so glad you're here,' gasped Lena between peals of laughter. Together, they swept up the shards of glass and, still giggling, half-heartedly dabbed the carpet dry. Then, share and share alike, they drank the other bottle of lemonade and ate the ice cream and all the other goodies and listened to the music together. All the while pouring their hearts out till everything didn't seem quite so bad after all.

Late that night, when Barbara stuck her head in the door to see if everything was all right with the girls, they were both sound asleep, arm in arm, with the music blaring. Barbara gazed over the picnic paraphernalia and drew her own conclusions. She turned off the music and put the light out with a smile, then she quietly closed the door.

15. Lena Earns Her Wings

School had started again and there was heaps of work to do. Even in the last few weeks before reports came out, the teachers still demanded a lot.

Lena wasn't able to spend as much time on the airfield as she had imagined. When she did make it, the weather was invariably poor. It was all very well helping with glider maintenance and parachute packing under supervision. She was working with the others and it was entertaining and even fun. Lena grew gradually restless though: she wanted to fly again.

It was the same for Martin. They usually got a lift to the airfield together. Their parents took turns. Sometimes Marianne, who lived nearby, picked them up on her way. Bolle and Maxl weren't there much. Presumably they had to put in an effort at school again, which actually suited Lena. She hadn't yet worked out how to get back on the natural, free and easy footing with Maxl that they used to have, so she preferred to stay out of his way. Martin was just like always though – and Lena soon forgot her misgivings towards him.

One Saturday she even went to a football match with Martin. Philipp's team were playing and Martin had once been in the team too. Since the cinema evening, Philipp and Isabella were no longer together. Lately, Lena, Martin and Philipp had all been getting on nearly as well as they used to before.

With Isabella though, it was more difficult. She alternated from being familiar and friendly on the one hand to caustic and catty on the other. Philipp ignored it and Lena didn't ask. He'd talk about it if he wanted to. She was just glad that he wasn't goading them about flying anymore. He was quite his old self again. Kim didn't know any more details than Lena. Her email contact with Philipp had faded away entirely. Instead, she kept up a constant stream of text messages with Bolle. She had also gradually made more friends in Berlin. Lena wanted to visit her in summer and was already excitedly looking forward to it. Philipp's team won and Lena and Martin celebrated with them.

Later in the afternoon, they all met up at Martin's place to study for a class exercise. Martin's room was covered in pictures of planes. Gliders on the airfield, in the air, in the mountains, upside down, from outside, from inside and in every conceivable size. 'Wow, I haven't been here for ages, does your room look like this too Lena?' Philipp asked.

'Nah,' laughed Lena, she was looking around curiously herself. 'My room's still just the same as it was. It's true though, I could have taken a few photos on the gliding camp! I totally forgot about it.'

'And? What did you guys think of the game? It was cool having you both there.' Philipp turned away from the photos and unpacked his schoolbooks.

'Well there was this ball and you all ran around a lot – it was really exciting…' grinned Lena.

'OK, I get it. You understand about as much about football as I do about flying,' Philipp laughed. He talked shop with Martin for a while about the game, the referees and who should have done what differently and where. Eventually they started on their work with a sigh.

The next day and the next two weekends, Lena had better luck.

The weather was halfway decent, and she was able to get back to training on the airfield. Stefan was there too.

Markus hadn't joined the club. He wanted to learn at larger flying schools during the holidays.

Maxl and Bolle were also there this time. Maxl was as affectionate as ever and Bolle asked Lena a lot of questions about Kim. She talked about Kim and how it had been before Kim moved to Berlin. Bolle was very curious. After a while, Lena's agitation subsided a little and she resolved to sound Maxl out. She was no longer content to tiptoe around him and keep upsetting herself in the process like an idiot. Maybe it was all a misunderstanding?

They pushed the K8 onto the runway for Martin. Bolle helped Martin get ready and Lena and Maxl went over to the Lepo to retrieve the cables. Lena hadn't quite got the hang of that yet. Actually, she tended to avoid it – she was happier recording the start times, but this time, her curiosity won out.

'Will you show me again how you retrieve the cables?' She asked Maxl. He held the car door open with exaggerated gallantry.

'It will be my honour,' he hammed it up. 'Do you guys have as much pressure at school as we do?' he groaned, when they were in the car. 'It's such a relief to be able to come out here on the weekends, otherwise I'd really go crazy.' He rolled his eyes dramatically.

'Aw come on, it can't be all that bad, you must still have a hot little girlfriend hidden away somewhere or other to take your mind off things.' Lena teased him coolly. At least she was outwardly cool. Maxl looked at her in astonishment.

'What gave you that idea?'

Lena turned to him.

'Oh, just saying…' she sidestepped the question nervously.

He grinned at her.

'Well who does like being alone? I had a visit from an old girlfriend not long ago. It was nice. Yeah… she's a glider pilot too by the way. Pity she lives so far away. Our parents are friends. You'd like her; she's a cool woman. Just like you. Next time she'll definitely have to come to the airfield. Could be a while till then though.' They had arrived at the winch and he sprang out of the car.

'Your turn, madam,' he called out jauntily. Lena wasn't sure if she should feel flattered or not. He thought she was cool, but what did his old girlfriend really mean to him now? Did he miss her? Maxl showed her how to hook the cables on again and Lena drove back. She had to take care to drive at a constant speed. She was so busy concentrating that she forgot about her questions. Later on she didn't dare bring it up again. Most of the time there were other people around and the intimate moment had passed.

She flew in turns with Piet and Fritz and they were both very happy with her flying. Lena was progressing well. In the evenings she and Martin were picked up relatively early. Most of the others stayed longer for a barbeque or just to chat. Lena missed the evenings around the barbeque. Paul had promised to come to the airfield for a weekend at the end of the month. Then she would be able to hang around for longer on the Saturday. Lena ardently hoped the weather would co-operate as well.

Unfortunately, it didn't, at least not fully. For July, it was quite cool and overcast. Paul confidently declared that it wouldn't rain though, so they drove out to the airfield as planned. Martin had even persuaded Philipp to come along that day. Now, on the way to Moorbach, Philipp was the only one in the car in a good mood. He had brought his camera with him.

Lena and Martin eyeballed the cloudy sky suspiciously.

'I wonder if that'll ever lift?' Martin yammered. 'We had such beautiful cumulus last week. You could have got some great photos THEN! But this?'

Philipp shrugged his shoulders.

'Why? It's not raining is it?'

Lena and Martin groaned.

'Don't be so melodramatic! You'll both get in the air soon enough. Be patient. Take the time to show Philipp around the place first – it might look totally different this afternoon.' Paul advised them. 'We're there.'

Despite the weather, quite a few people were already there, starting to unpack the hangar. Bolle was driving the winch out to the runway. Martin and Lena helped set up the launch point and did a daily inspection on the ASK21. The single seaters would come out later if the weather improved. Paul explained the operations and procedures to Philipp.

The weather wasn't up to much. Lena and Stefan trained circuits with Piet while all the others lazed around being bored at the launch point. The sky stayed overcast and it didn't look like it was going to burn off. The air was completely still. On her second landing Lena touched the ASK21 down gently, precisely on the threshold. She saw Martin and Philipp by the trees as she flew past. Philipp was taking some photos.

'Excellent, lassie,' said Piet in a satisfied tone of voice as he got out.

'So, let's say I pack up now and you fly the next few circuits solo, young lady.'

'What? Now?'

Lena had been completely distracted with other things and

hadn't thought of flying solo that day at all.

'Well, we just flew your check flight: Take off, good. Flying, likewise. Landing, perfect. I'm only ballast now, kid. OK?' Piet nodded encouragement.

'OK.' Lena's knees went wobbly.

They pushed the 21 back together. Martin and Philipp were telling her something, but Lena didn't listen to any of it.

At the launch point Piet gave Martin his parachute.

'We won't be needing that for now, put it over there!'

Martin looked wide-eyed.

'No way, really? Lena's going solo. Full-on!'

'What's up?' asked Philipp.

'Lena's flying alone for the first time. Today. Now,' explained Martin.

'Sick.' Now Philipp was flabbergasted too.

'Paul, go and pick some thistles, your daughter's flying solo,' hollered Martin in the general direction of the launch table.

'What, really, now?' Stefan looked offended. He wasn't ready yet. He still had problems with his landings. Paul swallowed and gave Lena two thumbs up from where he stood.

Lena took a deep breath and exhaled. Just don't get nervous now, she thought to herself. Everything's good. Piet wouldn't let me fly if it wasn't right. Taaaaake it easy. Piet fastened the harness in the rear seat, so nothing could foul the stick. Then he closed the rear canopy. Lena got in the front seat again and did up the harness. Piet squatted briefly beside her.

'So, no stress, little one. Fly another one just as calm and collected as those last two. I'll be with you on the radio just in case. You'll be fine.'

Lena nodded. Maxl came over with the cable.

'Ready for rope? Hey, wow, solo.'

Lena gave a wry grin and closed the canopy.

'Small ring.' Piet took the cable from Maxl and hooked on. Martin lifted the wing tip. Lena directed her concentration straight ahead. Take up slack... all out, all out... she chanted along with the procedure in her mind. Not so steep yet, now pull back... The ASK21 rocketed up. Ease off the backpressure, release, 380 metres, hmmm, now let's see, first a right turn...

'Good launch,' came Piet's voice briefly over the radio.

Lena's heart beat madly. She was flying alone! For a moment she turned around as far as she could in the seat and looked behind her. No one there. She had known it of course, but...

'Yeeeeeee-ha!' she cried, excitedly. She! Was! Flying! Alone!

Straight and level. Left turn. Right again. Smooth gliding. Quiet enough to hear a pin drop. Glance at the altimeter. 250 metres. One more turn. Downwind.

'Delta four six, Downwind,' she announced over the radio.

Locate the aiming point, base, unlock the air-brakes, final, check the airspeed, aiming point, air brakes, eyes to the horizon, gently coming back on the stick, landing. The flight was over before Lena had really grasped that she had been airborne.

The glider rumbled over the field and shortly came to a stop. She had done it! Her first solo.

Lena had to fly two more solo circuits. Only then would the first solo exercise, the A Certificate, be completed.

On the second launch she was quite calm. Amazing, she thought. A few weeks ago I didn't know anything at all about gliding and now I'm sitting here and get to control a plane on my own. I haven't even got a driving licence. Ha! That'll teach that conceited Isabella to be so arrogant. SHE can't fly. Even Philipp had given up mocking gliding and seemed to find it interesting enough to keep brandishing his camera around the place.

Lena took a deep breath and looked around almost reverently. The ground, school, day-to-day details, they were all so far away. Above her only endless sky, even if it was covered in cloud. Ahead, an ever farther horizon. The stillness. Here she was free! Free of anxieties and insecurities about other people. This was her thing. Here she could just be herself.

Lena savoured the feeling to the full. On the third launch she sang for joy at the top of her lungs. Just don't accidentally press the transmit button, she warned herself. The guys would laugh themselves to death if half the airfield heard me singing like this on the radio.

After her third landing everyone ran over to the glider, Paul and Martin in the lead. She had completed her A Certificate, the first Glider Pilot's Wings.

'Bravo, my little one!'

Lena had only just opened the canopy and had not yet got out when her father hugged her proudly.

'Papa, I can't breathe,' gasped Lena. Martin danced around the glider celebrating.

'Lena's done it, Lena's done it.'

'Yeah all right, we know, we were there,' murmured Stefan seeming irritated. Philipp took heaps of photos of Lena in the glider.

'So I did get the right day for photography. I knew it,' he said, winking at Lena. Lena grinned gratefully back at him. Now that the flights were over, her knees went weak again from excitement. Maxl helped her out of the plane with a grin and hugged her briefly.

'Fantastic! I knew you had it in you,' he whispered.

Then Piet was there and took her hand with a broad smile.

'So, my girl, now get yourself together. The others can push your glider back. You didn't expect that, did you? That you'd go solo today?'

'No,' admitted Lena. 'It was better this way. I would have died of excitement.'

'True, and this way you didn't drive yourself crazy and you flew as expertly as I expected,' praised Piet.

Nobody stayed sitting at the launch point. Everyone helped push or just walked alongside. Then came part two of the A Certificate. 'Now that we're all here, let's get straight down to action,' announced Piet as they arrived at the launch point. Before Lena could worry about it anymore she had to bend over a wing and let every person there give her a decent smack on the backside. Lena held her breath, but it actually wasn't so bad.

No one really hit hard except Bolle and Maxl.

'It'll give you a good feel for thermals,' they proclaimed loudly.

'Well, thank you,' grumbled Lena shortly. Then Piet pressed the traditional thorny bouquet into her hands. Ow, that prickled! But the elation won out.

'Lena, from all of us once again our heartfelt congratulations! May many, many equally awesome landings follow those,' declared Piet ceremoniously.

They all stood around *their* Lena for a while to be glad and rejoice with her. The weather didn't bode any better than in the morning. In fact, it looked like rain. No one was really keen on training anymore, so they decided to pack up and retire to the clubhouse.

The coffee machine in the club kitchen burbled away diligently, someone or other even rustled up some cake – and as the first drops fell outside they were happily celebrating. Lena made a quick call to her Mother to give her the great news and everyone nearby heard Barbara's enthusiastic yell.

Paul, Martin and Philipp disappeared for a while to the office in the tower. When they came back in, Philipp waved a couple of large photos.

'Ta-dah, hot off the press, Schoolgirl Flies First Solo,' he pronounced triumphantly.

'What's that? Let me see it.' Lena grabbed the pictures. In the office, Philipp had printed out some of the pictures he had taken earlier.

Maxl leaned over Lena's shoulder.

'Our Lena in her 21. They came out well, the pictures. Only here you look a little pale. A bit nervous maybe?' He put his arm around her shoulders and grinned. Lena glowed. She was embarrassed, but proud too. Philipp frowned. Lena gently freed herself from Maxl's embrace. As long as she didn't know where she stood with him, she didn't want to let herself be completely taken over by him again. Today was *her* day!

'Thank you,' she beamed at Philipp.

'I hope now you'll have at least one aircraft picture hanging in your room.' Philipp buried his hands awkwardly in his pockets.

'OK boys, let me in.' Paul pulled Lena towards him.

'All right my little one, um, maybe not so little. Your first Wings!' That said, he pinned a silver badge with a single set of white wings on a blue background to her jacket.

They all stood there. Lena felt as if she were in a dream. She would definitely have to call Kim tonight and report every little detail. Unless Bolle dared to relate any of it in advance; she would have to warn him off.

Lena looked around her, feeling very satisfied with herself and the world. It had suddenly turned into a really great day.

Paul, Piet, Maxl, Martin, Philipp, everyone was standing around with broad grins on their faces, nearly as broad as Lena's. She hadn't felt this good for a long time and the best thing was, it would keep going.

There were a great many weekends and holidays ahead of her that she could fly on. She would build on her new skills. There would be theory and radio lessons over winter. Next spring she might be able to fly cross-country and long distances. Maybe even with Maxl. Eventually she would take her friends and her family flying. She would see all her new friends often and Kim would sometimes be there too, at least in the holidays.

She looked dreamily at the pictures that Philipp had given her. Lena sighed happily. She had done it! She had earned her wings.

16. Summer Holidays

'Lena, dinner's ready!' Barbara stood at the foot of the stairs and called her daughter for the third time. She was gradually becoming annoyed. No answer came. She climbed the stairs with a sigh. It was the second last weekend of the summer holidays, Saturday evening.

She ignored the jumble of Lena's trainers, jackets, sun hats, and sunglasses, not to mention mountains of Jakob's toys that she passed on her way down the hall.

'Lena!' She opened the door. Lena was standing on the bed, barefoot, redecorating her bedroom wall. She was wearing headphones and humming along with the melody. Barbara could hear the rhythm clearly even through the headphones. Lots of photos and pictures of gliders lay strewn around her. A pile of clothes threatened to topple over on the foot of the bed beside a large rucksack and at least the same amount of clothes again were lying around wherever they had fallen in the room. Wardrobe doors stood ajar and the desk was a singular chaos of books, pictures and detritus including socks, sunscreen and sweets.

'What on earth happened here?' Barbara was now, officially, upset. 'Lena!' Lena still hadn't noticed her mother. Barbara plucked a sock from the bedside lamp and held it under Lena's nose. Lena whirled around.

'Mama! You really gave me a shock!'

Barbara snorted indignantly, 'Well, I did call you three times, and look at this place! You should have packed away your stuff from your week at Kim's ages ago. You're worse than your little brother – have a look out there in the hall! Everything just thrown on the floor! And your stuff from the airfield, too. We haven't had one meaningful word out of you since your holiday – morning, noon, and night, nothing but that racket in your ears.'

'OK, I get it!' Lena tried to placate her. 'I'm coming. I just wanted to quickly hang up the pictures. I'll tidy up soon, I promise.' She took off the headphones and had another critical look at her bedroom wall, then she brushed past Barbara on her way to the hall. Barbara remained sceptical.

'But after dinner, you're clearing up! Or don't think you're going to the airfield tomorrow,' she called after Lena.

'Yeah yeah! Of course,' rang out Lena's answer. She was already downstairs.

Barbara followed her daughter with a sigh. She never ceased to wonder at how Lena had changed in the last few months. How did the bookworm who had only seldom hung around with the neighbour's children or Kim become such an independent person? Of course, something had had to change after Kim moved away. Lena had been so sad. Gliding had come up just at the right moment. It seemed as if some boy must have turned Lena's head too – the headphones complete with iPod that Lena wore around everywhere constantly these days, certainly didn't belong to her. Besides, Lena's dreamy expression when she was listening to the music spoke volumes. Sometimes though, Barbara still asked herself what could be going on in her daughter's head.

Lena had spent part of her summer holidays in Berlin with Kim. The girls had been inseparable again, even though Kim now had heaps of new friends. Lena had been amazed and occasionally lost track of who was who. Kim had always been like that though. She was always at the centre of things. At the gliding camp she hadn't been an outsider for long and had quickly made friends with everyone, especially Bolle. Lena was afraid though, that Kim would soon find a replacement for Bolle in Berlin. Kim had once been infatuated with Philipp – that had been 'true love' too. It hadn't taken very long for Philipp to be ousted by Bolle. It would be the same again, Lena was sure – however much she might wish it otherwise. Hopefully Kim wouldn't forget her when she was out and about with her new friends. On the other hand, Lena had to acknowledge that she didn't have all that much time for Kim anymore either, what with all the gliding.

Why did everything always have to be so complicated? She missed her friend again already. She had to have someone to confide in about how things were going with Maxl these days. She and Kim had both found it so sweet of him that he had given her his iPod to take to Berlin. The music was really great too. There were a few love songs in the collection... Lena liked them the best. She actually wanted to be cooler and not so rapt to see him again every single time. She couldn't stand a repeat performance of him fooling around with that other girl somewhere or other and Lena herself ending up crying in a café toilet. No matter how much cooler she wanted to be though, it just didn't work. Her heart still beat faster whenever she saw him, and he had said he thought she was cool and... well who knows – maybe...? He had been really sweet again today – so uptight and nervous about his Glider Pilot's Licence test next weekend.

When they finally sat down at the dinner table, Barbara's mood slowly improved again. Lena talked about her training launches. Despite having her first solo flights behind her, she still had a lot to learn and had to keep flying with instructors. Barbara was always torn between being fearful for Lena and being proud of her daughter's achievements. Jakob on the other hand always listened rapturously to every word when Lena talked about the airfield. When it came to flying, he wasn't in the least ashamed to look up to his big sister.

'Next weekend they might let me fly the K8 for the first time,' Lena explained excitedly. 'Piet said if everything goes really well tomorrow, I can take the flight manual home for the week and check out all the details.'

'What will you take home?' interjected Johannes.

'The flight manual. Every aircraft type's a bit different. For example, the ASK21, that I've been flying up to now, is a composite two seater. The K8 is a single seater, so it's quite a bit smaller and a lot lighter. Just think how quickly I'll be in the air in that. It's sure to climb quite differently in thermals too. On the other hand of course it's quite an old model, built a lot chunkier and not as slippery as the 21... it feels really different to sit in. It's a high-wing type.' Lena was warming to her subject. Johannes smirked.

'I see!'

'Yes, but isn't it dangerous, darling? So soon? A new glider?' Barbara was immediately concerned.

'Aw Mama, the K8's supposed to be quite docile. And Piet must know what he's doing. Martin's been flying the K8 for ages and he isn't all that far ahead of me,' Lena protested.

'Lena will be fine,' Johannes tried to reassure her as well. 'I have complete trust in Piet, he even taught Paul how to fly.'

'Yeah, but you can't take me with you if you're flying a silly old plane with only one seat,' Jakob complained.

'I can't take you anyway, silly. Not till I've got my licence and that'll take nearly two years, until I'm sixteen. You know that,' Lena reminded him. When she saw his disappointed expression, she quickly added, 'You'll be the first person I do take though, when the time comes, I promise! I'll be able to fly all kinds of gliders later, not just the K8.'

'Yay,' Jakob rejoiced. He threw his arms in the air for joy, catapulting the piece of lasagne he had just skewered with his fork at the fridge...

Lena still had a long way to go before she got her licence though. In future she was supposed to work in the bookshop with her mother on some Saturdays rather than going to the airfield. She would contribute to the cost of flying with her earnings. Although Lena did think that was fair enough, she was concerned that she might not have enough time for flying. It would make little difference in winter, since it would be too cold to fly anyway, but Lena ardently hoped that some other solution would turn up before spring. Sometimes it was so difficult to stay patient. She wanted to fly!

The phone rang.

'Of course – always when we're eating,' said Barbara with a sour look. Lena had already jumped up.

'That'll be Kim.'

'Lena, we're eating! The answering machine'll get it,' her mother tried to check her. Lena was already in the living room.

'Relax, darling, let it go this time, it is holidays.' Johannes pressed Barbara's hand soothingly.

'Hm,' she didn't want to back down so easily.

'Lena, don't you forget what we agreed,' she called after her daughter in a strict tone of voice.

Lena reappeared in the kitchen with the phone to her ear, grabbed her plate, gave her mother an apologetic kiss on the cheek and disappeared into the living room.

'Mama, how long should I help in the bookshop next Saturday?' asked Lena when her mother came into the room before she went to sleep. Barbara looked around critically. Lena had tidied away her things from the passage and had brought the mess at least broadly under control in her room. Lena furtively pushed a pile of washing under the bed while Barbara was looking the other way.

'Well this is a good way to start, I must say. Why? You promised to contribute your share towards the flying, Lena. We talked about this.' Barbara sat down on the bed next to her daughter.

'Yes, and I really do want to,' Lena quickly softened her tone, 'only… next Saturday Maxl takes his exam for his glider pilot's licence. His birthday was last week; he's sixteen. The examiner is due at nine thirty and I would so love to be there. Please, please, please,' she begged. 'Maybe I could come to the bookshop a few times this week and only start doing Saturdays when school starts again?' Barbara considered for a moment.

'Fair enough,' she said in a more mollified tone, 'maybe it's a better idea anyway – otherwise you'll never be able to keep your mind on the job. It'll be a good way to learn the ropes. But I don't want to be having this discussion every Saturday and I don't care how good the weather, the thermals or whatever else is. OK? School comes first anyway! You don't have to fly all the hours for your licence in one year. The airfield will still be there next year. Do we understand each other?'

'Thanks Mami!' Lena hugged her mother impulsively. 'And Mami…'

'Now what?'

'Can I stay late on the Saturday night? Martin's allowed! And if it all goes well we want to have a double celebration: birthday and licence. Martin's mother will pick us up afterwards.'

Barbara chuckled to herself.

'You may. But the next day is a Sunday and you're staying home for a change and getting ready for school on the Monday.'

'You're the best.' Lena beamed.

'Yeah yeah, and when school starts there'll be no more of this gallivanting, do you hear? So, good night…sleep tight!' Barbara gave Lena a kiss and turned out the light.

Lena lay awake for some time dreaming to herself with her eyes open. Kim had told her on the phone that Bolle had invited her to the airfield on Saturday too. It was out of the question of course; Kim's parents would never allow it so close to the start of school. Berlin was just too far away. Pity.

Lena sighed. Kim had also been able to report that according to Bolle, Maxl's mysterious girlfriend wouldn't be there either… at least that was good news. Of course she could just have the same problem as Kim: too far away.

Lena resolved to subtly sound Maxl out again. The party would be a good opportunity. If Maxl had a close relationship with the girl, he would have to be disappointed if she wasn't there on the day. Kim had grilled Bolle for information about Maxl and his girlfriend, but hadn't been able to find out anything more. The only thing Bolle had said was: "You know Maxl!" That could have meant anything… or nothing.

Lena checked her alarm one more time. Set for seven thirty. Good. Her father would pick her up early tomorrow and take her to the airfield.

Hopefully the weather will be good, thought Lena. She was determined to have a couple more flights in the ASK21 and then sit in the K8 for a while to get used to it.

If it rained and the hangar wasn't unpacked, the K8 would stay hung up under the roof.

In that case she would have to wait at least another week before she could try out sitting in it. She wouldn't even be able to bring the flight manual home either, because it was always stored in the cockpit!

17. Airfield Heat

The next morning Lena was the first to wake. She slipped into her favourite jeans and fished the new T-shirt, that Kim had helped her choose in Berlin, out from under her bed. Some other clothes came out with the T-shirt. She quickly stuffed them back as far as she could. Hopefully, Mami won't get inspired and do a big clean up in here today, she thought to herself, as she dug out a pair of socks and headed off to the bathroom.

Five minutes later she was standing in the kitchen, spreading jam on a piece of bread and keeping a lookout for her father through the window.

Her mother appeared in the doorway, in her dressing gown. She was obviously not fully awake yet.

'Good morning dearest. Already on the go? Is the weather good for flying today?'

'Yeah, we'll see,' she mumbled with her mouth full. She washed the bread down with cold milk.

Barbara sleepily switched on the coffee machine.

'Do you need…'

'Papa's here,' Lena interrupted her. She left everything where it was lying and ran excitedly to the front door. 'I have to go. Bye Mami, see you tonight.'

'Wait, don't you want to take something to eat?' Barbara tried to detain her for a moment and followed her daughter into the passage.

'No time, there'll be something or other there.'

Lena gave her mother a sloppy kiss on the nose on the way past, grabbed her airfield bag and flitted out the door.

'Ewww – not like that. You know I don't like it,' Barbara dried her nose with the back of her hand. 'Have you got everything?' she called after Lena.

'All here!' Lena patted her bag. 'Hat, sunglasses, sunscreen, logbook – the rest will turn up. Ciao Mami.' Lena blew her mother a kiss and got into her father's car. Paul turned the car around, tooted one last time, and they were off. Barbara stood in the door a moment longer, waving.

'It's always the same! Airfield days – raring to go in the mornings, school days – not so much,' she sighed and went back to the kitchen.

Paul and Lena picked Martin up on the way to the airfield. He was already outside waiting for them.

'Hi Lena, morning Paul.' Martin flopped into the back seat behind Lena.

'So, Martin, you haven't drunk too much coffee for breakfast I hope, in case the weather's good?' Paul joked in greeting. Lena grinned.

'Ha ha, very funny,' Martin defended himself half-heartedly, 'but the weather will be good today. This time for sure. I'll do my five hours today.'

'You can do it,' laughed Paul.

'As long as you leave me the flight manual. I want to fly the K8 too next week,' said Lena. She turned to face Martin. 'And if you bomb out, I'll fly the five hours before you.' Lena grinned at him.

'Would you listen to that! Success is going to your head young lady. Fly solo for a few days first…' Paul grinned, ruffling Lena's mop of curls affectionately.

'Oh Papa,' scolded Lena. 'Lay off!'

Martin scratched a small pimple on his chin.

'Yeah, yeah, of course I'll leave you the manual. You can take your time getting used to sitting in it this morning. It's not so warm yet. It might take a while till the thermals get going. What do you think of the pictures from the gliding calendar? Was there anything there you could use?'

'I hung them all up except for two,' said Lena with a smile.

When they got to Moorbach Airfield twenty minutes later, the big doors on the hangar were already open. Piet and Marianne were supervising the unpacking of the hangar. Maxl and Bolle were standing beside their mopeds in the car park. Maxl had tousled hair as usual, as if he had just rolled out of bed, and Bolle had a freshly styled haircut.

'Who are you trying to impress today? Are we expecting visitors? Kim's in Berlin, isn't she?' Martin mocked with a sidelong glance at Bolle's head.

'Ha ha, very funny, you could at least have washed *your* hair,' Bolle defended himself with a grin. He wasn't so far off the mark either. Greasy hair, pimples and glasses – that was the Martin they knew.

Martin studiously failed to hear him and sprinted off to get "his" K8 out of the hangar. Bolle followed him. Marianne waved to them impatiently.

'Where have you been?'

'And are you already nervous about the exam next week?' Lena asked Maxl.

He casually laid an arm over her shoulders and they slowly ambled across together to join the others.

'Don't tell anyone – it's actually really easy, nothing, I've done it hundreds of times already and Fritz has thoroughly briefed me. Again.' Maxl whispered to her. 'But I'm terrified – No idea why, I'm not usually such a scaredy cat with exams, but this time…'

'Do you two lovebirds need a personal invitation today? Lend a hand both of you, or you can copy out launch lists in the tower for the rest of the day,' Marianne berated them loudly.

'What's up with her today?' Maxl wondered. He let go of Lena and grabbed the K8 dolly. Without the dolly, it wasn't possible to get the glider out of the hangar.

Martin stood next to his glider in the hangar looking rather embarrassed. The K8 hung from the roof in two loops. He had let it down with the winch, but forgotten to put the dolly underneath first. A glider undercarriage is fixed and not steerable and since the K8 hung sideways in the hangar and there was no room for manoeuvring, Martin and the glider were pretty well stuck. Marianne rolled her eyes, looking irritated.

'For heaven's sake Martin. Typical! Lift the K8 up again with the winch. You won't get it out that way. Really, it's not as if it's the first time you've done it!'

'Easy now – no harm done,' Piet reassured her. The old instructor and Lena glanced at each other questioningly – what was with the ratty mood? There really was no harm done.

They all helped lift the K8 back up a little, Maxl placed the dolly under the main wheel and then they could easily roll the glider out of the hangar sideways. Marianne had already stormed off again to the next plane.

'Typical female: nought to hysterical in three point seven seconds. Everything OK?' Stefan came around the corner acting markedly casual. He had a cup of coffee in his hand and was still enjoying his breakfast roll.

'You here already?' Now it was Lena's turn to roll her eyes in annoyance.

Always the same banal sayings, especially from Stefan.

Bolle rapped him on the head with a knuckle as he passed. Stefan jumped, and dropped his bread roll.

'Look out, idiot!' he snapped at Bolle.

Bolle and Maxl grinned at each other conspiratorially across the glider.

'Right, that'll do! Take the gliders out to two seven please; we've got a westerly. At the double!' Piet resolutely put a stop to the bad tempered argy-bargy in a tone of voice that showed he wouldn't put up with another word.

A short while later, the K8, the two-seater ASK21 and three other gliders were collected at the glider launch point on runway two seven, inspected and ready to fly. The winch, at the other end of the airfield, was also ready.

Lena and Stefan had to practice modified circuits, and landing from unusual positions. That was important so as to be able to land safely from a low height in case the winch cable broke. Also, you might need to outland on a cross-country flight and not have as much space as normal. Piet described all kinds of situations and how to react to them. Lena yawned furtively. When Piet was finally finished with his briefing, she wheedled:

'Can I fly later? Stefan can go first. I want to sit in the K8 a bit to get used to it.'

'The K8 isn't going anywhere, and Stefan got here last today – you're going first,' said Piet decisively.

'Oh OK,' grumbled Lena and started getting ready.

Piet was ambitious. Lena had to launch five times. Every time he manoeuvred her into a different unusual situation. Every time she had to make quick decisions and work out how to land the glider safely. It wasn't easy. One time Piet released the cable just after they took off. She had to bring the nose of the aircraft down smartly from the nose high launch attitude to the normal flying attitude and land straight ahead. That was a critical situation where you had to react quickly. They proceeded in the same style. Sometimes Piet had to intervene and help her when she didn't immediately know what to do next. Lena groaned one time when that happened.

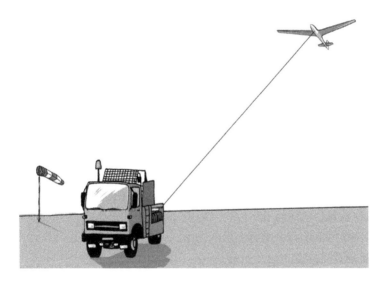

'We'll practice that again this afternoon – otherwise you won't be flying the K8 next week.' Piet obviously wasn't satisfied yet. Then it was Stefan's turn.

'Don't worry about it,' Maxl reassured her at the launch point, 'it'll turn out all right.' Lena nodded, mollified.

'You're not flying today? she wondered.

'Maybe later. Haven't got the nerve.' he admitted, sounding subdued.

'You really are nervous! I wouldn't have expected that from you. You're usually so confident when it comes to flying! Bolle's always green with envy.'

'Really? I never noticed.'

'Yep. He'd never admit it in front of you of course, but it gets to him sometimes that you flit away and leave him behind, even though you started flying at the same time back then.' Lena explained.

'Ok, I'll watch out for that. I didn't want to put his nose out of joint – but on the other hand everyone's making such a fanfare now. "You'll get through, we'll all have a big party," everyone ALWAYS expects Maxl to make it – and what if I don't?'

Lena didn't know how to answer that. She looked wide-eyed at him, astonished, and just took his hand in silence. He squeezed her hand in answer, cleared his throat briefly and took up the radio to announce Martin's launch in the K8 to the tower.

By now, some thermal activity had started. Marianne was already underway in the LS4, Bolle had grabbed a glider and left, Stefan and Piet were flying the same exercises that Lena had done earlier and Martin was impatient to start his new attempt to fly five hours continuously in the K8.

'Well, it looks like I won't be sitting in the K8 till tonight,' sighed Lena resignedly, 'at least he left the manual.' She ran over to Martin to hook his glider on and run the wing. 'Good luck!' she called to him.

There was one more glider waiting to fly. After they had launched it, Maxl took the Lepo to retrieve the cables. In the meantime it had got really warm; the thermometer had climbed to 26 degrees. Lena got a bottle of water from the launch point bus. It could turn out to be a long day. There wasn't a cloud to be seen in the sky – a blue day – Piet had called it. Phew! She fetched a couple more shade umbrellas and set them up around the launch point table, otherwise people would be roasted alive here today.

That's how it turned out too. The single seaters stayed up and Lena had to take turns with Stefan at practicing modified circuits. It had become an arduous endeavour now that the thermals had made the air so much gustier. Hours later, they were all soaked in sweat and fed up. Piet let Stefan land long and taxi up to the hangar.

Bolle was already back too. Lena, Bolle and Stefan scrubbed the dead insects off the leading edges of the glider and carefully washed the canopies with a chamois. Lena would have preferred to tip her bucket of water over her head. So hot! It was now over 32 degrees Celsius.

'I wonder how Martin's going in the K8? His five hours will be up soon.' Bolle scratched irritably at a particularly tenacious splattered fly, puffing and blowing. 'The air may be a lot cooler up there, but the sun will still fry your brain. I hope he took his sun hat, and something to drink.'

Stefan toiled away at the other wing. He groaned dramatically.

'Well, I've had enough for today anyway. It's a real scorcher.'

The three of them and Piet stowed the clean gliders in the hangar. The winch was packed away. No one wanted to take any more launches. Marianne landed too, visibly pleased with herself. She pushed her glider off to the side near the trees and brought the parachute and battery away with her. Then she joined them, sipping from a large bottle of water.

'I feel better now. Are you all still talking to me? Sorry I was in such a bad mood earlier. It was a terrible night; the baby wouldn't stop crying. I was wasted this morning.'

'Don't trouble your poor head about it lassie, already forgotten,' Piet yawned lethargically. 'Now we can all lie in the shade and count down the minutes till our dear Martin can land. In 26 minutes he will have done it.' Tired and sweaty, they all searched out shady spots for themselves.

18. Crash Landing

Lena sat on the ground and leaned against a birch tree. From there she had a good view of the circuit area and the runway. She flipped the pages of the K8 flight manual half-heartedly. In fact she was much too lethargic for studying. Martin was soaring to the north of the runway, still relatively high.

'He's got it good,' she sighed enviously. If only she was up to that stage too. She did have some respect for the challenge of flying a new aircraft type though. It wasn't so long ago that she had started flying at all.

'Do you want me to quiz you?' Maxl was standing there, pointing to the spot beside her. All the others had long been sitting down nearby. Lena's heart skipped a beat.

'Ummm… sure!' She held the manual out to him. Maxl took the little folder and flopped down on the moss beside her with a relaxed sigh. He gave a gaping yawn. Then he laid his head across her lap as if it were the most natural thing in the world and stretched himself out.

'Sooo: maximum aerotow speed is…?'

Lena awkwardly plucked a few blades of grass. She had no idea what to do with her hands. Even if she had picked up a few points from the manual, she was pretty sure none of them would come to mind *like this*.

'Ummm… Hmmm – to be honest, no idea, I haven't really absorbed much yet…' she stammered nervously.

'No problem, that's what you've got me for,' declared Maxl

jauntily. 'It's quite simple: never exceed speed is 190 km/h, but in rough air, only 130. Aerotow is 130 km/h too and on the winch it's 100, OK?'

'190 km/h, 130, 130 and 100 on the winch,' Lena murmured, trying to concentrate despite how close Maxl was. She had swapped from blades of grass to plucking at his tousled red hair and to her surprise it felt quite natural and relaxed. She would never have believed it, and with everybody here too! Maxl was in a good mood, quoting more and more facts and numbers about the K8. Lena felt quite contented. She could sit and study like this for hours! After a while they heard Piet talking into the hand held radio.

'Congratulations Martin; the five hours are up. You can come down and land now.'

'Finally, the klutz managed it,' grinned Maxl.

'Look! He's in a hurry to come down now; full air brake descent with steep turns,' Lena pointed to the circuit area.

'I think you mean a full bladder descent,' said Maxl, tongue in cheek and sat up. Everyone got up and watched Martin in the circuit. He called late downwind on the radio.

'Isn't he still a bit high? Or is it an illusion?' asked Lena.

Piet was already on the radio again.

'You're too high Martin. After a long flight the perspective can trick you. Have a look at your altimeter! Don't turn base yet!' Martin gave a double click on the radio in acknowledgment.

'Not particularly talkative at the moment, is he?' Marianne wondered to herself.

Martin extended his downwind leg. Piet was satisfied again. Eventually, Martin turned final, opened the airbrakes fully and lined up on the runway.

'Well, he'll be pretty pleased with himself anyway,' grinned Bolle.

Piet ran forward a few paces to get a better view.

'You're pretty low now boyo, brakes away again or you'll land in the middle of nowhere. Concentrate on your speed!' he ordered over the radio.

'What on earth has gotten into him?' he wondered. Martin didn't react.

'Oh no, don't be stupid now man,' murmured Maxl nervously. Lena swallowed apprehensively. She was suddenly afraid for Martin and had a lump in her throat. Everyone had jumped up now and they were all straining their necks for a better view. Marianne grasped Lena's hand and held on frantically.

'Come on, come on, come on, do it!' Bolle willed Martin, his gaze fixed on the K8.

'Brakes. Away!' Piet commanded emphatically over the radio.

It looked like Martin was just about to hit a large hazel bush that was normally far enough away from the runway that it didn't cause any problems. At the last moment he slammed the brakes away and pulled back on the stick. The K8 shot up over the bush. Everyone ran forwards, concerned. They all watched breathlessly.

'EASE the stick forwards!' Piet bellowed into the radio. The K8 climbed a formidable distance into the air and rapidly lost airspeed!

'Much too slow! It'll fall out of the sky! That's how you stall,' cried Maxl anxiously.

Martin had apparently reached the same conclusion. He slammed the stick forwards. The nose dropped and the K8 tilted steeply down and sped towards the ground. Piet swore.

'GRADUALLY pick it up,' he coaxed Martin over the radio,

unfortunately in vain. As Martin once again headed steeply for the runway and the ground came up at him impossibly quickly, he panicked. He jerked the stick abruptly back and pulled brakes at the same moment. That was too much for the K8.

The airflow over the wings broke away once and for all – and they stalled. With no remaining forward momentum, the K8 flopped down hard from three metres up. The tail came down first on the grass before the runway. Then the fuselage impacted.

For a moment everybody was dumbstruck. Then they ran to the stricken aircraft.

'Martin,' Lena howled anxiously. Piet fiddled with the canopy, trying to open it.

'Martin, are you ok?' Martin sat speechless in the K8 and didn't move. His face was bright red and he was soaked in sweat. His hands were trembling.

'Come on kids, give me a hand here!' Piet had opened the canopy and handed it to Bolle. Meanwhile, Marianne was calling an ambulance and Martin's parents.

'He's in shock. Let him sit there for a while in case he's injured his spine. Lena, get some water – Martin's burning up,' ordered Piet. Lena flitted off and found a water bottle in her backpack.

Less than ten minutes later though, when the ambulance arrived, Martin had already clambered out of the cockpit and drunk a little water. Now he was hunched over in the shade, running his fingers through his hair anxiously. His initial speechlessness had given way. He apologised to Piet over and over with tears welling up in his eyes.

'It was so hot and I forgot my water and my hat, but then everything was going so well! And then it was so cold again on my feet and then I thought, not so bad... and... but the K8, can it be fixed? Imagine how much it'll cost. It's bound to be stupidly expensive. And I've never been *that* bad at landing.'

All the while Piet tried to calm him down…

'Nobody's born an expert, drink some more water, kid – calm yourself down! Your old instructor could have looked after you a bit better too, couldn't he? It's not the first time you've been running around here without a sun hat. If anyone messed up, it's me. I was responsible. Come here, everything's OK! Your parents will be here any moment.' Piet was quite remorseful himself. He took Martin gingerly in his arms.

The paramedics said Martin had a mild heatstroke – he could count himself lucky that the symptoms weren't worse. He should drink lots of water, get some sleep and stay in the shade. As long as he didn't throw up or get a bad headache, everything would be OK. Lena was relieved. She had never seen her friend so distraught. It was lucky nothing worse had happened!

Martin's parents arrived to take their exhausted son home. Piet went to the car with them and explained exactly what had happened.

'My brave little scatterbrain.' Martin's mother looked Martin in his overheated face with concern. 'I'm sure he'll take more care in future, when he gets into a glider. I'm so glad you were with him!' She thanked Piet again, then they hurried off. Piet scratched his head thoughtfully and slowly walked back to the spot where the K8 lay.

'Bolle, Maxl, how's it looking?' He looked over the boys' shoulders with a furrowed brow. The two of them were busy inspecting the K8 from every possible angle and looked sceptical. 'There are deep folds in the fabric at the tail. The fuselage is badly bent too,' called Bolle, sounding very serious.

'It's going to be heaps of work, better be prepared for a long winter,' Maxl portended.

'Hmmm,' muttered Piet, 'this doesn't look good, we'll have to get an expert to look at it. If we've got actual kinks in the steel tubes – well, we can save ourselves the effort. It's not worth it!'

'Whaaaat?' Lena didn't believe her ears. 'What'll happen to the K8 in that case?' She looked at Piet in panic.

'Well, unless I'm very much mistaken, this plane has had it, it's simply a write off! The old girl is just too old. We'll do better to buy ourselves something newer and more appealing with the insurance money. A professional will know more – I really can't say! Take the K8 to the workshop now please; I've got a lot of phone calls to make. See you next weekend.' Piet tapped the old aircraft twice on the tailplane and plodded off towards the tower.

Lena couldn't take it in.

'But, but…'

'You're just going to have to wait, princess. Piet's not going to let you convert straight to the '19 or the LS4. That's the end of any hope of flying a single seater this year. You'll get another chance next season,' said Bolle cuttingly. He had hit the nail on the head. That was precisely what Lena was afraid of. She didn't want to show any weakness in front of the boys now though, by shedding a tear.

'Leave Lena alone,' Marianne joined in. 'Let's go! Push! Tail first! To the hangar!' Lena nodded to her thankfully and picked up the wing to help.

19. Friends?

The next morning at nine o'clock, Lena was in her mother's bookshop, with a stack of boxes in front of her.

'You see, it's quite simple – top up the display stock. The postcards and decorations are in the boxes, it's obvious which cards go where, and you can be a bit more creative with the decorations. Just put out whatever suits the book tables, OK?' Barbara cheerfully handed her daughter a knife for opening the boxes and turned her attention to a customer, who had just entered the shop.

Lena nodded compliantly. Her thoughts were miles away. She thought about Martin's unfortunate landing with mixed feelings. On the one hand she was naturally glad that nothing worse had happened. On the other, she was actually quite upset: did he really have to crash the K8, now of all times? The one aircraft type that she was allowed to convert to so far. Mami hadn't been exactly relaxed about it either, when Lena had told her about the accident last night. Luckily Paps had come to Lena's aid and employed all his powers of persuasion to help reassure her mother. Incidents like this, he had said, were the exception rather than the rule and in this particular case sadly typical for a scatterbrain like Martin. How could he have been so thoughtless as to set out to fly five hours in that weather without water or a hat? Lena would be much more sensible. In the end, Lena's mother had calmed herself down.

There was the party on Saturday to look forward to as well. Lena could hardly wait. She was absolutely certain that Maxl would pass his test. If only it could be Saturday already! The week stretched out endlessly before her. She checked her phone again; still no answer from Kim. Hadn't she received Lena's text from last night? Lena had briefly described Martin's accident and wanted to get so many other stories from the airfield off her chest and share them with Kim. Nothing. Lena was planning to visit Martin in the afternoon and see how he was doing…

'Lena, are you dreaming? Hello? Earth to Lena? The postcards are all upside down. Do them again please, and get it right this time!'

'Oops – sorry Mami,' Lena quickly packed her phone away again and checked over the postcard stands one more time.

Later, she and her mother drove home for lunch.

'That wasn't so bad after all, was it? Tomorrow you can run some errands; we deliver a few books to older customers. They'll be glad to see a new face,' Barbara prattled away cheerfully.

'No problem,' Lena plugged an earphone back in her ear and checked for the umpteenth time whether Kim had messaged her. Nothing doing. Such a fair weather friend; Lena was gradually getting annoyed with Kim. Last week we were doing everything together and now, not a peep.

'Are you even listening to me?' Barbara waved her right hand in front of Lena's face.

'Um, I'm running errands tomorrow, right?' Barbara had said more, but Lena hadn't been listening. 'Something or other about Frau Mayer…?' Barbara rolled her eyes.

'OK, for the second time…'

In the afternoon Lena stood at Martin's front door with a huge box of chocolates. There was still no news from Kim.

Martin's mother opened the door.

'Hello Lena! It's nice of you to drop in, that'll cheer him up. He's been stewing in his own juice all day.'

Martin was in his room, sitting on the bed and staring gloomily at a pile of aircraft magazines on his lap.

'Hey, how's it going?' Lena bumbled into the room. The air smelled musty and stale. Martin's face briefly lit up when he saw Lena, then he twisted his hair remorsefully.

'I crashed your K8, why are you even still talking to me?' Lena couldn't stop herself letting out an involuntary laugh at all the theatrics.

'Come off it! It's not my glider. And it could have happened to anyone.' She sat down cross-legged on the other end of the bed and tore open the box of chocolates.

'Here, chocolate is good for the nerves.'

'Things like that don't happen to anyone except me. No one's that muddle-headed! Even my own mother says so. I don't feel like chocolate, thanks,' replied Martin sourly.

'Pull yourself together! Gliding's a team sport. You've hammered that into me often enough, remember? We were all a bit soft around the edges yesterday, and it's no wonder in that heat. We could have asked you before you launched if you had everything... or afterwards on the radio,' Lena tried to reassure him.

'Exactly – with anyone else, you'd never even think of it. Maxl never forgets his water or anything. Marianne doesn't even get out of her car on the airfield without her hat. The hero of stories like that is only ever dopey old Martin. Now they'll never let me fly again, just wait and see.' Martin was so distraught, there were actually tears in his eyes.

At that moment his mother came into the room with the phone.

'It's for you. Piet wants to talk to you.' She opened the window and went out again.

'Hi,' mumbled Martin quietly into the phone. 'Yes. Better. Yeah, thanks. No. I'm so sorry… but I did though. Am I allowed to… yes. OK… OK… thank you! Yes, Lena's here now. Will do. Yes. See you Saturday and – thanks!' The conversation may have been short, but Martin's expression looked a lot more relaxed afterwards.

'I am still allowed to fly. First up, Saturday morning. Before Maxl's exam. In the 21, with Piet of course. He says, when you fall off a horse, you have to get back in the saddle. Phew!'

'Well, what did I tell you? You're not giving up that easily. We won't let you,' Lena tried to cheer him up a bit more. She shoved a piece of chocolate into her mouth and held the box under Martin's nose. He took a piece.

'But really Lena, I thought they'd throw me out.' Martin took a deep breath. 'You've all been so awesome. I mean, you wanted to fly the 8 so badly and now you have me to blame that you can't and…' Martin looked at her bashfully, swallowed and ran his fingers through his hair. 'I was so totally swept off my feet when you suddenly appeared on the airfield back then and we just got on so well and understood each other straight away. You know, normally, girls never talk to me like that, and when you actually came to the gliding camp too, well…'

Martin's face changed colour from a pale to a deep pink and his ears glowed bright red. Oh – no. In one moment Lena abruptly realised exactly where this conversation was headed. She had only wanted to cheer her club mate up in a purely friendly way. Why was he suddenly sweating so much, all over again? She wanted to curl up in a ball and hide. Had Kim been right the whole time?

Right on cue her phone vibrated in her pocket. Lena looked at the display. Message from Kim: 'EVERYTHING OK? HOW IS MARTIN?'

'That's Kim – she wants to know if you're OK,' Lena made a feeble attempt to steer the discussion in another direction.

'Oh thanks, say hi from me,' Martin was pleased, but he wasn't going to let himself be distracted. Having once plucked up the courage, he wasn't going to be held back now.

'Lena, well… I – what I wanted to say is, maybe you realised already, but when you drew your hand away that time on the runway, I didn't dare anymore, I wanted to…' he stammered.

'Martin,' Lena didn't even want to let him finish. She nervously mangled the next chocolate in her hands. 'I'm really sorry, I didn't want to… I mean, flying is just so great, and everything was so new for me, I didn't realise that you… well… can't we just be friends?' she blurted out.

'Oh. OK. Oh well. I should have known. It was silly of me. I…' Martin swallowed, disappointed.

'No, it's my fault, I'm so sorry,' Lena hastened to add. What a disaster. Things really weren't going well for Martin at the moment. She was truly sorry for him.

'You're keen on Maxl, right? Of course I can't compete,' Martin declared, sounding frustrated.

Lena blushed now and had to take a deep breath. It was getting worse and worse. She wished the ground would open up and swallow her. She had no idea what she should say.

'It's understandable… but wasn't he out with some other chick recently, going to the movies? Ahhh, so that's why you disappeared so fast that night.' Martin stared at her, surprised at his own insight.

Lena didn't know whether to laugh or run away in shame. 'So, it's not so straightforward for you either, is it?' Strangely enough, the thought seemed to reassure him. Lena burst out laughing in spite of herself.

'Wow, Martin, you're a strange one.' She couldn't stop laughing. Martin looked baffled, then he started giggling and finally they were both bent over double with laughter.

'It'd be tragic if it wasn't so funny,' he gasped.

When they had calmed down to some extent and gathered up all the chocolates that had distributed themselves all over the room in the outburst, Lena solemnly offered him her hand.

'Friends, anyway?'

'Friends!' Martin nodded, relieved, and gallantly shook her hand.

'But promise me you won't tell anyone, OK? Only Kim knows,' Lena entreated coyly.

'Yeah, yeah, I know. Girls! You shouldn't have to ask.'

'And you're really not upset?' Lena probed, despite herself.

'I'll survive,' Martin wheezed, 'you know, when you fall off a horse…' and they howled with laughter again with their mouths full of chocolate.

At that moment the door opened again and Philipp came in.

'What's going on here? Am I interrupting?'

'Hihihi, no, haha, sit down, have a chocolate, they're good,' Martin giggled.

'I have to go.' Lena stood up, taking the opportunity to leave before it got embarrassing again.

'I didn't want to scare you off,' Philipp countered helplessly and looked from one to the other.

'Is something wrong?' he asked suspiciously 'Won't you stay?'

'No, everything's fine – I really should go. Ciao Martin, see you on Saturday. Ciao Philipp – see you soon.' Lena hurriedly left the room. The boys watched her go with regret, but she didn't notice; she was gone.

What a story! Kim had better answer her phone now.

20. Girl Trouble

'Kim? Finally! Why haven't you called? You'll never believe what's been going on here.' The words bubbled up in Lena when she finally got Kim on the line.

'I was out, I'll tell you all about it when we have more time. I've gotta go again soon, party at the youth centre, should be really great,' replied Kim. Lena thought she sounded rather distant.

'Oh, I see… well, if I'm disturbing you…?'

'Nah, 'course not, tell me about it! It's terrible; did Martin really crash?' Kim was obviously making an effort to show a bit more interest and enthusiasm.

'Well you wouldn't really call it a crash, just a terrible landing 'cos he had heat stroke – he was really wasted. And now the plane's written off. My K8! I would have been allowed to fly it as my next type – it's a real pain, I tell you.'

'Oh, is that all? I thought it must have been something really bad.'

'Didn't you hear me? The plane is completely done for. And can you imagine how Martin's taking it? It's killing him. And that's not even the worst bit. You won't believe it. I dropped in on him just before, to see how he was going and he suddenly got all sentimental on me, he was on the verge of making a declaration of love. You were right, he's completely infatuated with me. It was so embarrassing!'

'How come? – It was pretty obvious!'

'No! He was like, stammering it out and I was like, trying to get him to stop and then he twigged that I'm actually into Maxl. But he promised me he'd keep it to himself. That was really nice of him…'

'Oh my goodness, what a drama! You should try giving him a chance; maybe you'd suit each other after all,' replied Kim dryly.

'Now what's that supposed to mean?' Lena's cheeks were glowing.

'Nothing, calm down, hey – I have to go. Talk again in the next few days? Everything worked out all right in the end, don't worry about it. OK, till next time,' Kim hastily ended the conversation.

'Bye, talk soon,' Lena tried to say, but Kim had already hung up.

Lena was disappointed. Annoyed even. The call had not gone the way she had imagined it, at all. Kim didn't even think it was bad that the K8 was broken and that Martin was distressed, quite apart from Lena herself. And what about her revelations? It wasn't nothing, whatever Kim might say about it. Ok, Kim had had to go, but her *best friend* really hadn't sounded particularly interested. And who was she going to that party with? Last week, when Lena had still been visiting Kim, there hadn't been any mention of it. Lena didn't know whether she was more angry or sad.

That night, she lay awake for a long time pondering these remarkable developments. The only good thing was that Martin had reacted in such a relaxed way in the end. Hopefully it would stay that way in future, otherwise it would be awful for both of them at school and on the airfield.

On Saturday there'd be the party too. They were supposed to get a lift to the airfield together and be picked up in the evening by his mother. She swore to herself that she wouldn't let anything spoil *that* day. Lena plugged Maxl's music into her ears. That did help, even if nothing else did. She lay awake for what felt like hours and eventually fell asleep.

Lena spent the rest of the week, more or less, with her mother in the bookshop, even though there wasn't really all that much for her to do there. She might as well earn some brownie points while she could, seeing as how she had no other plans anyway. She hoped it might encourage her mother to be a bit less strict on the weekends in future.

Kim hadn't been back in touch, and Lena still felt slighted over their last phone call. She wasn't going to run after Kim this time. She would have to look after herself. It was always Lena who had to call. That was over. Lena felt sad about it and checked her phone more and more often, but no message came.

Something strange happened towards the end of the week. Lena was out running errands for the bookshop. There were a couple of cookbooks to deliver to Frau Lamprecht, who was in hospital. Low fat cuisine; well if it helped…. With Maxl's music in her ears as usual, Lena crossed Bahnhofstrasse and turned the corner. The next moment she sat down hard on the pavement, still holding her books.

'Hey, can't you look where you're going!' she complained as she got back to her feet. The girl who had run into her helped her up.

'Isabella!'

'Head in the clouds again?' Isabella retorted in an unfriendly way.

'Not at all,' Lena started to defend herself, although she wasn't totally sure whether Isabella's reproach might not be justified. 'Sorry, I didn't see you, but you did shoot around the corner too.'

'Maybe. Sorry.' Isabella's manner stayed brusque.

'Everything OK?' Lena persisted. 'How were your holidays? We start again on Monday, I wish we had longer, don't you?' Isabella frowned.

'The usual. Normal holiday with my mother. Hours and hours in the car. Dull as dishwater. Katy's got no time either. She's got a new boyfriend; just doesn't respond anymore. Absolutely fantastic holiday, really. What about you? Airfield dreams all come true?' she answered, sarcastically.

Lena instinctively took her ear buds out, feeling a little guilty. 'It's been cool. Visited Kim in Berlin, went flying at the airfield.' She didn't want to go into further detail. Isabella seemed quite grumpy. 'Not doing anything with Philipp anymore?' Lena let her curiosity get the better of her.

'Huh!' snorted Isabella, 'YOU'RE asking ME! You don't get anything, do you? I've gotta go, see you round.' With that, she was gone. Lena watched her go, feeling perplexed. What was *that* supposed to mean? Had Kim kept something from her that time after all? Maybe she should push Philipp for more of the story next time she saw him. It was getting stranger and stranger. Lena continued on her way, deep in thought.

The week stretched out forever. The bookshop couldn't really hold Lena's attention for long. She was so looking forward to the party.

Saturday finally arrived. The weather wasn't anything to write home about – stratocumulus Piet called it – quite dense overcast. At least it wasn't supposed to rain. It was still very early when Barbara dropped Lena and Martin off at the airfield. Martin was nervous. He couldn't get last week's terrible landing out of his system. Lena did her best to distract him, telling him about her strange encounter with Isabella. Try as she might though, she couldn't get more than "Hmm, yeah strange, hm hm" out of him. His thoughts were somewhere else entirely.

They weren't the first to arrive at the airfield. Piet and Marianne had already got the ASK21 out of the hangar, Maxl was attending to the winch, and Bolle came around the corner carrying two parachutes.

'Have fun today, you two. Martin – I'll keep my fingers crossed for you, it'll be all right.'

'Thank you Frau Reisenberg,' answered Martin mechanically and slunk over to Piet and the two-seater apprehensively.

'Oh the poor dear! I feel really sorry for him – Lena, look after him a bit today, won't you? See you tonight; his mother's going to give you a lift after the party. Well, bye my little one.' Barbara blew Lena a kiss and drove off. Well, that would suit him down to the ground, if I started mollycoddling him now. Maybe not too much of that, Lena thought to herself, sauntering over to the others.

'Best of luck Maxl! Is the examiner here already?' she called to him.

'Hi Lena. No, they asked him to come later, because of Martin.' Maxl's face looked particularly pasty this morning.

'Here – this is for you,' she valiantly pressed a small, plaited, plastic wristband into his hand. Lena had agonised for ages over whether she would really dare offer it to him, and now she held her breath involuntarily. Don't be such a chicken, she chided herself inwardly.

'What is it?'

'Jakob, my little brother, made it for me once, as a lucky charm for a particularly nasty maths exam. It worked, I got an A.' Lena fixed her gaze on her shoes.

'You're so sweet, thanks! That's really kind of you, nothing can go wrong now, can it?' Maxl gave a wry smile and kissed her briefly on the cheek. Lena blushed and glanced furtively over to the group by the 21. Phew. Luckily, Martin hadn't seen anything.

'Listen up everyone, we'll get straight into it so we'll be ready when Maxl's examiner gets here,' called Piet loudly and clapped Martin on the shoulder. 'I'm only ballast, kid, you can do it! Everyone push, tail first, let's go.'

Lena, Bolle, Martin, Marianne and Piet pushed the ASK21 to the launch point. Maxl took the winch to the other end of the airfield and Bolle drove the Lepo, to tow out the cables. There was a tense feeling about everything, but everyone stayed calm and focussed. Fritz, Stefan and a few others gradually drifted in.

Lena helped Martin on with the parachute. Piet got into the back seat of the 21. He seemed quite relaxed and calm. Even though the sun wasn't shining, Martin was wearing his bucket hat. He wouldn't make the same mistake twice. He took a deep breath and climbed into the plane.

'You'll be right!' Lena nodded encouragingly. When he was ready, she hooked on the cable, went to the wing and waited for his signal. Martin gave the thumbs up and Lena lifted her arm.

As everyone (except himself) had expected, Martin flew three perfect circuits.

By the time they were pushing the glider back after the last landing, he felt a lot better. Only his red ears still betrayed how agitated he was.

'So, boyo – broken the ice again?' Piet amicably pulled Martin's hat down over his nose.

'Yes – thanks.' Martin sighed with relief and shoved his cap back on his head. 'All good.'

'Well then – Maxl's examiner has arrived, so, on with the program.'

They pushed the 21 back to the launch point and left it to Maxl, Piet and the examiner.

Maxl had to answer some questions about various parts of the glider and do another daily inspection on it. Lena kept her fingers firmly crossed. Then they got straight into it, and an hour later they were all back at the launch point again, shaking hands.

'Congratulations on your successful Glider Pilot's Licence exam, young man. I hear you're a talented cross-country pilot too. I think we can expect great things from you,' the examiner praised Maxl.

Finally the tension eased in all the others as well. The whole crew had been holding their breath for Martin and Maxl since the early morning and now they celebrated exuberantly. Lena had only wanted to congratulate Maxl and give him a quick hug, but he lifted her off her feet and spun her excitedly around in a circle.

'Yesss! Yee-hah,' he rejoiced. Everyone beamed. Lena got quite giddy. Piet pulled out the scissors.

'I hope you've got a proper shirt on, young fella m'lad, 'cos you're about to lose your collar!' He cut Maxl's shirt collar off and held the trophy up high with a laugh. Everyone clapped. Then they went to the clubhouse. Everyone was in need of refreshment after all the excitement.

There was a party atmosphere in the clubhouse. Litres and litres of coffee and cocoa were passed around. Maxl's mother had confidently supplied a cake for everyone. Maxl thumbed out messages on his phone like a man possessed and accepted congratulations from all directions. Some other treats were already prepared for the evening.

Martin was in a good mood again and much more talkative.

To Lena's relief she was able to gossip and chat with him just like normal; there were no problems between them. After everyone had eaten their fill and quieted their initial agitation, they all went back outside again.

21. Long Landing

The weather hadn't got much better, so Piet and Fritz took turns flying with them in the ASK21. Martin took a few solo launches in between. Lena had a few turns too, but she wasn't really concentrating on flying. She kept seeking Maxl out. She was boundlessly happy for him. He was now in such a good mood that his head was full of nonsense. He decorated the Lepo with dandelions and wildflowers, until it looked like a hippy van.

He took a turn at the launch table, where he sang crazy songs down the telephone to Bolle, who was driving the winch.

His radio calls might have been more suited to a Wild West comedy show than an airfield.

Maxl chased Marianne and Lena all over the airfield and tried

to roll them down a slight slope in a couple of old tyres. Piet smirked.

'Yeah yeah, once they're let loose on the world, look out! But this morning was a different story, wasn't it?' The girls shrieked playfully and gave him a taste of his own medicine. He was thoroughly tickled, stuffed into the tyres and rolled down the hill. He lapped it all up.

Evening was approaching, time for the hangar flight. 'It's never the *last* flight, only ever the *hangar* flight,' said Piet solemnly, just as he always did. Lena was supposed to fly the hangar flight today. It meant a long landing and taxiing up to the hangar doors and they were only allowed to do it with an instructor. It was always a fun flight, so whoever got the chance always jumped at it.

'So, Lena, make your final approach like always; just use a lot less airbrake. We don't want to touch down so early this time. I'll take over at the end,' Piet instructed her before the landing. Lena looked at the aiming point and continued on downwind. Out of the corner of her eye, though, she kept watching Maxl and the others packing things up at the launch point and heading off towards the barbecue area…

'Hello? Would you care to turn in now? I'd prefer not to land in these trees. Concentrate!' Piet snapped at her suddenly. Oops, bother! She had been so busy watching that she had flown much too far out without noticing.

'My aircraft.' Piet informed her brusquely that he was taking over control. He turned right sharply. They were now much too low for a normal approach with a base leg and a long final. Lena's heart raced. Piet lowered the nose markedly and picked up speed. The airfield was on a slight rise and Piet was now aiming at a point below the field. They were flying very fast now. Lena swallowed.

If they crashed another plane now because of her... please, anything but that. She was terribly ashamed. It was almost like what had happened with Martin. Just before the bushes at the edge of the airfield, Piet pulled up and used the speed of the ASK21 to gain height. Lena was pushed down hard into her seat. They shot over the bushes with only metres to spare, Piet levelled the aircraft out and pulled brakes, then they gently touched down. They were at the other end of the airfield from where they had expected to land though, a long way from the hangar and the clubhouse.

'So much for a long landing! What was going on in your head, Lena? We don't daydream while we're flying! I really wouldn't have expected that from you.' Piet clambered out of the glider and looked at her questioningly. 'Imagine if that had happened to you in the K8. You'd be hanging from the treetops over there right now. Not a smart move, young lady.' Lena opened her canopy, trembling. There were tears in her eyes.

'I'm so sorry,' she stammered. She couldn't bring herself to utter another word. She could see Maxl, Bolle and Martin getting underway to help them push. This was going to be embarrassing.

'Come here child.' Piet helped her get out. 'I didn't mean it like that. Maybe I expect too much from you all sometimes... there there.' He waited patiently until she had taken a deep breath and calmed down again. 'That really was a landing from an unusual position and that's all they need to know... OK? And next time you can show me again that you really can do it, is that a deal?' Lena looked up at him thankfully.

'That's a promise!' She swore to herself that she wouldn't disappoint him.

'What was THAT?' she heard Bolle call.

'That, young man, was a Piet Special and I'll thank you never to try it yourself,' countered Piet with a grin, and that was the end of the subject. They all pushed the ASK21 back to the hangar. Lena felt weak at the knees, but nobody seemed to notice.

Stefan was waiting for them outside the hangar.

'Botched the circuit, did we?' he smirked.

'You're just jealous because you didn't get the flight,' Martin defended Lena. She said nothing – Stefan was right!

By the time they finally finished packing everything into the hangar, the large barbeque had been fired up by a couple of retirees. Maxl's parents had arrived with alcohol-free strawberry punch and lots of goodies to eat. Aside from that, the boys were

busy building up a huge campfire a few metres further along. Benches and tables came out and were set in a circle around the fire.

'Listen up everyone,' Piet called out. 'Before all your growling bellies descend on this wonderful spread before us – a big thank you to Maxl's parents by the way   Fritz and I want to make an announcement: We've had a fantastic season, you've all worked really hard and learnt a lot. We're both very proud of you and before your holidays come to an end, it's time to reward you young people. Marianne, a round of desert schnapps for our heroes if you please!' Lena, Stefan, Martin, Bolle and Maxl all looked at each other questioningly. What did he mean? Schnapps? He couldn't really mean it! Maxl's parents just grinned. They must have been in on the secret. Something didn't smell right. Marianne came out of the clubhouse carrying a tray, and it really did have five shot glasses on it. They were full of something light-coloured.

What was going on?

'You can't be serious,' said Bolle sounding incredulous. He was the first to cotton on. They took a glass each. Lena sniffed hers carefully. It was… it was bread crumbs. Oh, well that can't be all that bad, she thought to herself feeling relieved.

'Bottoms up!' commanded Piet. '…and cheers!' They all tipped their desert schnapps into their mouths as one. For a moment, nothing happened. Then they all tried to chew or swallow and their eyes widened in surprise. Martin couldn't help coughing and a huge cloud of dust issued from his mouth. Maxl laughed and promptly started coughing too. The adults laughed themselves silly and the other three sniggered restrainedly, at least as much as they could with their mouths full of bread crumbs.

'Say gross national product!' Marianne challenged Bolle with a grin.

'Gwoff… noff- now… ppp' the rest was drowned amid peals of laughter.

They laboriously chewed at the dry mass for some time. Maxl was the first to get his mouth halfway clear.

'Water,' he gasped. The second tray, with glasses of water, was laid out ready.

'Wow, that's nasty stuff.' Martin tried to dislodge the last residue from between his teeth with his tongue.

'It dries your mouth right out, you wouldn't believe it,' Lena laughed and greedily drank a great gulp of water.

'My friends, you have come through your baptism of fire, or should I say baptism of breadcrumbs? I now declare the buffet open,' Piet grinned broadly. They loaded up their plates with sausages, salad, baked dates and lots of other good things and found themselves places to sit by the fire.

The setting sun gradually turned the sky pink.

'Lena, you can go flying now; your sky,' Stefan pointed up. Lena wanted to open her mouth to make some retort, but no snappy reply came to mind quickly enough. Maxl glared at Stefan fiercely.

'I'd cut the stupid talk if I were you.'

'Or what?' Stefan snapped back. 'Her knight in shining armour will jump in and rescue her? Oh, the poor helpless damsel in distress!'

'Oops, sorry, were you still hungry?' Marianne artfully stumbled with a glass of punch in her hand and the contents spilled all over Stefan's plate. His pile of sausages with ketchup was completely soaked. A good part of the resulting sausage soup swashed into his lap. Stefan sprang up in disgust.

'Hey!'

'Oh, did you wet yourself?' asked Maxl impassively. Fritz sauntered past; he had seen everything.

'Stefan, you should know by now that this lot are as thick as thieves. Whatever you were up to, I wouldn't try it again. Go and change into something dry, there's an old pair of overalls in the workshop somewhere,' he grinned.

Stefan skulked off. 'Was that really necessary?' asked Fritz, addressing everybody. He was obviously struggling to hold a strict tone of voice.

'What do you mean? The sausages must have still been hot, and now they're not,' said Marianne with honey in her voice. Fritz went away again shaking his head. Marianne winked at Lena.

It quickly got dark. Everybody was pleasantly surprised when Fritz unexpectedly produced a guitar from his car after the meal.

'Hey, hidden talent? Why didn't you bring that along to the gliding camp?' wondered Piet, looking pleased. Fritz started playing straight off – and he was really good. He even knew *Flieger grüß mir die Sonne*. Everyone sang along.

They sang lots of songs about flying. It was getting late. Lena, Maxl, Bolle and a few others danced wildly around the fire. Lena was glowing. It did still bug her that the landing had gone so badly, but right at that moment her worries were a very long way away. Maxl was dancing around beside her, holding her hand and grinning at her, the music was great, the fire was cosy… everything was really good. The next song was more sedate and most of them flopped back down on the benches. Maxl gently led her a bit further into the darkness outside the pool of light from the fire. Here, the others could hardly see them.

'A little bit further,' he whispered. Lena followed him. She felt her heart fluttering.

He stopped suddenly, and she very nearly ran into him. She was about to take half a step back, but he held her tightly. The others were only vaguely audible. She was now standing right up close to him.

'I'm so glad you were here today,' he whispered. He smelled of strawberry punch and campfire. She would have dearly loved to see his face, his eyes. Then he gently felt for her face, lifted her chin – and kissed her. Really kissed her. Lena could hardly believe it was happening to her, now. Just like that! She felt warm and cold all at once, she felt her heart beating, everything seemed to tingle! She was on cloud nine. Although – everything felt right! Didn't it? Were they going out together now? What was the story with that other girl lately? Why did she have to think so much while they kissed? It wasn't supposed to be like that, was it?

'Maxl, I…' she began half-heartedly and tried again to make out any expression on his face in the darkness. No chance.

'Shhh…don't speak, just enjoy it,' he kissed her again. She couldn't have said how long they had stood entwined in the dark until Martin suddenly turned up with a torch.

'Lena? Oh there you…' The word stuck in his throat. Oh no, not now, thought Lena, feeling somewhat dazed. There was a moment of embarrassed silence.

'My mother's here, sorry!' He seemed to be honestly embarrassed.

'I have to go,' Lena gave Maxl one more kiss. 'Will you call?'

'See you round,' returned Maxl coolly and kept on waving as she followed Martin to his mother's car.

'Are you going out with him now?' Martin asked her quite directly in the car.

'Um, it looks like it,' answered Lena, somewhat taken aback. Was he angry now? 'I think so,' she added for good measure. She wasn't sure what to think. 'Are you angry with me now?'

'No, I just wanted to know,' Martin sighed dramatically. 'But be careful with him!'

'Why?'

'No idea, just a gut feeling.'

'Well well, so you've got a gut feeling – are you sure it's not just that Bolle slipped something into the punch?' Lena grinned. Since when was Martin such an expert on relationships?

22. Another Crash Landing

At home, later that night, before she fell asleep, Lena checked her phone over and over. She was hoping for a message from Maxl. Did he even have her number? In any case, it shouldn't be too hard for him to find it out. She was still tingling. He had really kissed her. He liked her. She couldn't wait to tell Kim! But no, waiting a bit longer would be better, there'd be sure to be more to tell. Otherwise Kim would only make fun of her again. Should she send Maxl a message? What would she write? She reached for Maxl's music again with a sigh.

It was very late when she finally fell asleep. When she woke up, there was no message. After breakfast: no message! After three games of memory with her brother: no message!! After she had tidied up and packed her school things: no message!!! It bothered her more than she wanted to admit, even to herself.

Fair enough: Maxl would have to be at the airfield today, clearing the remains of the party away, she thought. Maybe he'd left his phone at home. She quashed the thought of writing to him off her own bat. She'd see him in the morning at school anyway. She imagined the looks on her classmate's faces when they realised she was going out with Maxl. Especially Isabella, who always acted so mature and looked down on everyone. Now Isabella was alone for a change and Lena had a boyfriend.

Lena couldn't help quietly gloating to herself.

Midday, afternoon and evening all came and went: still no message. Lena went to bed impatiently early that evening.

Tomorrow couldn't come soon enough.

'What's up with you? Are you sick?' her mother wondered. 'You're going to bed already?'

'I'm fine, I'm just tired. Good night Mami, good night Johannes.' She gave each of them a good night kiss and made herself scarce. Johannes and Barbara watched her go in amazement.

'Miracles do happen. She'll probably be reading under the blankets till midnight,' Lena's mother speculated.

'Or, more likely, she'll be chatting with her friends,' grinned Johannes.

'Ah, you're right, I'll have a look and see what she's up to later.' However they were both mistaken. When Barbara went upstairs an hour later, everything was quiet in Lena's room. She wasn't reading or chatting, she was fast asleep dreaming about a boy with tousled hair...

Naturally, she kept an eye out for Maxl at school the next day. Most of her classmates were already inside; she was the only one still moping aimlessly around the yard. Had she missed him, was he already inside? Eventually there was nothing for it; she had to go in. She slipped in to the classroom at the last moment, practically in the teacher's wake. There was one spot left, right in the back corner next to Philipp. OK, here goes! Martin shrugged his shoulders at her and gave her a questioning look. Of course he actually knew exactly why she had waited outside so long. Lena made a face and flopped into the chair next to Philipp.

'Hi,' she whispered. 'Can I?'

'Of course, where else would you sit?' he whispered back. There was no more time for pleasantries; the new teacher, Frau Böhmer, was pointedly staring at them. She had a reputation for being unforgiving and very strict. It wouldn't be smart to attract negative attention in the first five minutes. Frau Böhmer announced that she'd be taking them for Maths and Social Studies as she handed out the lesson plans. It promised to be no end of fun.

The new teacher lived up to her reputation. After a few organisational points, she plunged straight into calculating square roots. Lena tried intently to follow the explanations, but her thoughts kept drifting off.

'Finding the root is the inverse of squaring a number,' Frau Böhmer droned on. Beside her, Philipp gave a quiet sigh and secretly rolled his eyes. Lena answered with a wry smile.

'Is there a problem back there? The holidays are over, good people!' Frau Böhmer had scarcely interrupted her speech, only pausing briefly to give them a hard stare over the top of her glasses. Everyone looked back at them. It was deathly quiet in the classroom. This was crazy; they hadn't even done anything that bad. Lena and Philipp stuck their noses deeper into their books and said nothing. The woman was infuriating. They hardly trusted themselves to look away for a moment until the bell rang. The class was finally over and Frau Böhmer swept out of the room.

'Uugh,' Philipp breathed out audibly. 'This'll be the death of me. I can't stand it. What a dragon.' Lena nodded. She already had her jacket half on and was hurrying to get outside again.

'What's the big rush?' He looked at her questioningly. 'Cat got your tongue?'

'Your darling's not here,' Martin suddenly butted in, before Lena could say anything.

Lena froze.

'Martin! What...? Why...? Couldn't you shout it any louder?' She looked around uncertainly to see who else, apart from Philipp, had heard everything and pulled Martin aside. Great, now Philipp was frowning too. 'You promised to keep your mouth shut. What's going on? And where is Maxl then?' She hissed.

'How come I have to tell you? I thought you were so intimate?' Martin was making the most of the situation.

'Well?' Lena was in no mood for jealous games.

'Oh, the school's got an exchange program this year, so Maxl's class is starting school ten days later than normal. He's been raving about it for ages. Manchester. And then the English kids will be here, with us, at school for ten days. Host families and so on, you know.' Martin's expression was obviously sympathetic.

'Oh! Right, I see,' she said feebly. She couldn't manage to say anything more. Lena was dumbfounded. Yes, he had said something about it sometime or other, but she had had no idea that it was actually happening now. Why hadn't he mentioned it again? She sat back down feeling deflated. Philipp looked at them both questioningly, but neither made any move to explain anything to him.

'Your boyfriend?' he persisted, in Lena's direction. Martin nodded absentmindedly in her stead.

'Ah ha?' Philipp responded, sounding distinctly cooler. 'I'm off to get some air.' He grabbed his jacket and headed outside.

Martin looked at Lena apologetically.

'I really didn't mean any harm or anything, I thought you knew about it.'

'Nothing you can do, all good, thanks,' she murmured gloomily.

'OK, good. That's that then. I want to go outside for a bit, before the dragon starts spitting fire again, are you coming?' That was the end of the story for Martin.

'Nah, you go on, maybe I'll be along in a while.' Martin shrugged his shoulders and went outside. Lena stayed behind on her own.

Why hadn't Maxl said anything when they parted at the airfield? *See you in two weeks* or *I'll miss you* or, well, anything at all? Why hadn't he been in touch again before leaving for England? Did he think she knew anyway? Wasn't there a need to clear things up regardless? Whatever he might be thinking, it wasn't enough for Lena. She decided that texting him now was out of the question. He would be busy with his host family, British school, and who knew what else. Deep in thought, she chewed the end of a pencil feeling dissatisfied. In the meantime, the bell had rung and her classmates had come in again. Philipp sat next to her in silence, but Lena was too sunk in her own thoughts to wonder about anything. Before long Frau Böhmer came in again too, and her strict regime picked up where it had left off. Lena still couldn't concentrate. Earlier, the problem had been anticipation, now it was disappointment gnawing away at her. Were she and Maxl together or not? Everything didn't fit together somehow. This wasn't what she had expected at all!

The first few days back at school were Lena's toughest and worst ever. She was disappointed by Maxl's lack of commitment, but she hadn't yet completely given up hope; maybe there was a good reason for everything. She was frustrated about the bad landing and Kim's lack of interest – and on top of that there was the new, strict teacher. Altogether it was just a bit too much.

She tried to pull herself together, at least in class, so that she wouldn't lose the thread completely, but her confused feelings were just too strong and they distracted her too much. At home she argued with her brother more and more often. His perpetual good mood really got on her nerves. Everyone was so nice and concerned and wanted to help. Her mother, Johannes, Martin. They could tell immediately that something wasn't right. Of course, Martin also knew what wasn't right. They all meant well, but whenever they said anything, it got on her nerves so much… Couldn't they just leave her alone? Did she really have to be cheerful all the time? She wanted to work it out herself, she just didn't know how. Somehow she had the feeling she had got out of step with the world. Mami's soothing words were no help. Then there was the weather. A deluge. She could forget going to the airfield on the weekend – what a pain! There was only work and Mami's pitying expression to put up with all Saturday. Several times over the weekend, Lena sat down at the computer and composed a long email to Kim, but every time she deleted it again. Somehow she had lost the connection to her old best friend. Lena had pretty much known it would end up like this sooner or later, once Kim had found lots of new friends. After coping so well over summer though, the end of their intimate relationship seemed to have come very suddenly.

Lena did what she always did when she was sad: she read. Until Wednesday of the following week it was nearly impossible to talk to her. She brooded around with a gloomy expression on her face and kept her nose in some book or other. Unfortunately, as Frau Böhmer once pointedly remarked after a look at Lena's homework, not her maths book.

Thursday morning before class, Lena was standing expectantly in the schoolyard keeping watch again. Maxl had to be back today, either with the exchange students or without them. Either way she could at least talk to him, however briefly. Maybe then she would finally know where she stood.

Sure enough, after a while she saw him, with a large group of students she didn't know, drifting towards the main entrance. She took a deep breath and ran up to him. Even if she made a complete fool of herself, she had to know, now.

'Hey sweetie, how are you?' He called out to her cheerfully. Lena peered at his wrist. Was he still wearing her armband? With the long sleeves on his jacket, she couldn't tell. 'We're in a bit of a hurry, meeting with the exchange people and all the teachers, you know? See you round!' Maxl gave her a friendly grin and a short, non-committal clap on the shoulder on the way past, then kept moving along with the group.

That was it. That was definite. Wasn't it? He didn't care about her at all. Lena had opened her mouth to reply, but now she shut it again. For the life of her, she didn't know what she could possibly say. She just stood there. Her eyes burned as she tried to hold back the tears. She had known the whole time, of course. What was she doing still standing here? Maxl had long gone, disappeared into the building with the others.

It suddenly occurred to her how quiet everything was around her. Oh no! How long had she been standing around in a trance? She had to get inside. Lena ran off. She opened the classroom door tentatively.

'Ah, Lena! How nice of you to grace us with your presence,' Frau Böhmer upbraided her and made herself a note.

'Sorry,' murmured Lena, blushing strongly, and slunk to her seat with slumped shoulders. Philipp didn't make a sound. Frau Böhmer continued the lesson, giving out exercise books. Lena still had a huge lump in her throat. She would have preferred to go home straight away, but with this strict teacher, she didn't dare. What should she do?

Somehow she managed not to get upset for the rest of the school day. Well, at least mostly. Luckily, in Frau Böhmer's class they only had to work on exercises in the books, so she didn't have to talk to anyone. After that they had two hours of art; easy. At the end of the day they had French with Monsieur Laponte – he liked the sound of his own voice more than anything. In the breaks, Lena avoided Maxl. She was much too agitated. She wanted to be at least tolerably composed when they talked to each other. Once, Martin did point out that Maxl was standing just over there by the noticeboard, in case she was looking for him. However Lena stopped Martin with a wave of her hand, so he kept his thoughts to himself and left her in peace.

In the bus on the way home, Philipp made an attempt to entice her out of her reserve. He sat in the seat behind Lena and leaned over the seat-back to talk to her.

'So, what's up? Is Böhmer getting to you? There's really no

point getting upset about it – she's just like that.'

'Hm, that too. Things haven't been going that well lately. At the airfield and that, as well. Hasn't Martin told you about it?'

'No, he only talks about his launches and landings, clouds

165

and weather forecasts and who knows what...' grinned Philipp, trying to cheer her up. 'Anything I can do to help?' He fiddled awkwardly with the seat cover in front of him.

'Thanks. Nah. I wouldn't know what.' Lena pulled one of her books out of her schoolbag absentmindedly. She didn't say anything else. Philipp obviously couldn't think of anything else to say either; he gave up.

'Oh well, in that case...' he said resignedly and sat back in his seat.

At home in her room, she could finally give herself up to the tears. Eventually her mother came in and took her in her arms. Lena sobbed, blubbered and sniffled. Everything poured out of her and finally she told the whole story. She told her mother about the terrible landing, the wonderful evening around the campfire, the kiss, the waiting and finally about her huge disappointment. Barbara didn't say anything at all at first. She just listened and handed Lena occasional tissues. They stayed huddled together, talking for quite a long time and gradually Lena settled down a little. Jakob put an end to the serious mother-daughter talk in his own peculiar way: he burst into the room, threw himself onto the bed between them and bawled – completely senselessly, but all the louder for that – at the top of his lungs:

'The mouse was sick, the mouse was sick, now it's whistling again, hooray, hooray!'

'That - doesn't - rhyme - at - all,' Lena gave her brother a wry grin and tickled him, first his feet, and then all over. Jakob squealed with delight. Barbara joined in and tickled them both until they lay still, cackling with laughter and fully worn out.

'Come on Jakob, leave Lena in peace for a little while, you can play downstairs.' Barbara and Jakob left the room again and Lena stayed behind, feeling tired. She was still sad, but talking about it had done her good. On the spur of the moment, she followed her mother downstairs to the computer, so she could finally send Kim an email. All of a sudden it was quite easy, and if Kim thought it was silly or childish, that was her problem.

23. Paint Damage

Lena may have talked away her woes and even got Kim involved, but the feeling of relief didn't last all that long. Somehow she was still smitten with Maxl, regardless. That kind of feeling couldn't just be turned off, and the disappointment gnawed away at her all the more. Didn't the kiss mean anything to him? Did *she* mean so little to him? There was no word from Kim. Lena kept dragging herself to school feeling totally frustrated and unmotivated. Philipp did try to cheer her up or distract her, but Lena remained taciturn and eventually, he gave up. They sat next to each other at school, but apart from the bare necessities, they hardly spoke. Lena completely failed to realise how withdrawn and uncommunicative she appeared to everyone else. Her verbal participation in class reduced to an absolute minimum. She was deep in her own world and busy with her own problems.

The weather didn't exactly help brighten up her mood either. It was proper autumn weather, complete with rain and storms. Not airfield weather at all. Great.

The only one who seemed not to take Lena's bad mood seriously was Martin. He talked non-stop just like always. He followed her around in the breaks wherever she went and didn't ask silly questions if Lena abruptly changed direction when she saw Maxl somewhere. Maybe he was still hopeful? After a while though, she ruled that out. Martin seemed to be happy just to have someone he could talk to about flying.

He was even able to persuade her to go to the airfield with him on Sunday despite the bad weather:

'Don't you want to find out what the inspector said about the K8?'

'Definitely – do you think it's really had it? But then what will happen? Surely they won't let the trainees get straight into the LS4 after the 21?' Lena speculated pessimistically.

'Nah, I don't think so either,' Martin agreed. 'Maybe we'll get a new plane?' His eyes gleamed in anticipation. There was no trace of a guilty conscience on account of it being his fault that the K8 couldn't fly anymore.

'We'll see, maybe Piet will already have the dates for workshop duty and theory lessons. Surely there won't be much more flying in this weather. At least not in gliders.'

'You're right there,' acknowledged Martin sounding downcast. 'It's going to be a long winter. Five months and no gliding! How am I supposed to hold out that long?' he groaned.

'Do you want to grind out circuits in the winter cold?'

'Nah, but the aerobatics pilots are still flying heaps, when it's not actually raining… and cloud base is high enough.'

'You could help push,' Lena ragged him, 'only licenced pilots with heaps of experience fly aerobatics.'

'Yeah yeah yeah… I know,' muttered Martin. 'You're working with your mother again on Saturday, right? We'll pick you up on Sunday morning then. Maybe your folks could take us home?'

'I'll ask and give you a call,' Lena acquiesced with a sigh. She wondered whether Maxl would also be there on the weekend.

The English exchange students hadn't left yet. According to Martin, they were supposed to set off on Tuesday. She wasn't sure if that was a good thing or not.

On Sunday, they drove to the airfield as planned and met Piet in the workshop. As expected, the weather was bad. There was hardly anyone else there. Marianne was pottering around somewhere in the hangar repacking the parachutes.

'Ah! Two volunteers! Good to see you here,' Piet really did seem pleased to see them. He was working on one of the motor gliders. It was up on jacks and disassembled for its annual inspection.

'Here, hold this,' he handed Lena a screwdriver and disappeared under the fuselage.

'Piet, has the inspector been for the K8?' Martin's curiosity wouldn't let him wait.

'Yep,' Piet crawled back out from under the fuse holding the motor glider's nose wheel.

'Flat. Puncture.' he announced, scratching his head. 'We've got another one around here somewhere.'

'WELL?' Lena pressed him now too.

Piet looked at her earnestly.

'Done for. The steel tube fuselage is bent, actual kinks in the tubes. You can see it in the fabric, folds all over it. It'd be too expensive to fix. It's not worth it. It was a pretty old aircraft after all.' Lena and Martin looked at him in shock.

Martin swallowed.

'Will I have to pay for it now?'

Piet laughed,

'For heaven's sake, Einstein, no. That's what we have insurance for. I've already explained it all to you and your mother. We're shopping around at the moment – maybe we'll get a nice ASK23 in spring.'

'Really?' Martin was instantly brimming with enthusiasm.

'Is that something like a K8?' asked Lena.

'Nah, more like a single seat 21,' he beamed. 'That'll be cool!'

'Yeah, *LIKE – TOTALLY COOL!*' Piet aped him with a grin. 'But only if you both get in and help here.' Between them they managed to fit a new wheel to the motor glider. Then they had to take out the seat pan, inspect the control circuits and grease them in places. All the connections had to be measured to see if there was too much play anywhere. Piet was qualified to oversee the maintenance and he carefully watched everything that Lena and Martin did.

Just then, Maxl came into the workshop with another boy.

'Andrew, this is Piet, our gliding instructor and some friends from school, Lena and Martin,' he introduced them. Maxl spoke English; Andrew must have been one of the exchange students. Andrew shook hands with everyone. Piet straightened up and stretched his back.

'Maxl, can you show these two how to sand the damaged section of the leading edge? Then mix up some gel coat, put it on and get them to sand it again, after it's hardened. You've done it a few times before, right? I need a coffee break.' That said, he left the workshop.

'OK,' Maxl puffed himself up and showed Lena and Martin what they had to do. He gave Lena a familiar wink in the process. Martin rolled his eyes.

'We'll be fine with it, I've done it before too,' he snapped at Maxl.

'Ooh – sensitive today, aren't we?' Maxl let them sand the wing in peace for the time being and turned his attention back to his guest. Andrew was looking around curiously and seemed happy enough.

Maxl called Lena over to the paint cupboard.

'This is the gel coat. You have to mix it up and then put it on thinly with the brush, later it can be sanded and polished. Lena stood nervously in front of him. Why couldn't she just switch off her feelings?

'Everything OK? Lena?' Lena had been staring at a spot on the floor. 'Is this about the other week?' he whispered, sounding concerned.

'Well, I thought, you know...' Lena dithered about.

Maxl didn't let her finish.

'We're still friends though, right?' He looked at her with his most charming smile. 'Here, you'll be fine!' He handed her the gel coat and before she could say anything (not that she would have had any idea what) he turned around and left the workshop. He took Andrew with him, to show him the planes in the hangar. Lena watched him go, feeling bewildered.

'Such a braggart,' Martin grumbled. 'As long as he's the big hero, that's the main thing. Give it here, what do we have to do?'

'Brush it on and sand it again later,' Lena mumbled vacantly. 'Didn't you just say you've done it before?'

Martin blushed.

'Oh yeah, well I watched once...'

They got on with the job with enthusiasm. It wasn't particularly warm in the workshop, so after applying the gel coat, they went to the clubhouse to have a drink and warm themselves up.

'So kids, is it all done?' Piet asked.

'Yeah, just has to dry,' replied Lena. They sat with him for a while. Marianne was finished with her parachutes and was also treating herself to a coffee. After three quarters of an hour Piet herded them back into the workshop.

'So, let's have a look at your handiwork.'

Maxl and Andrew were standing casually beside the motor glider. Stefan stood by as well, trying to polish his English skills.

'Maxl, has the gel coat hardened? Can we sand it?' asked Piet.

Maxl touched it carefully with his hand.

'Eww! What's that then?' He looked at his sticky fingers with distaste. His fingerprints could clearly be seen in the spot where he had touched the gel coat. 'Why hasn't it dried?' he scolded.

'Maybe it's too cold in here?' speculated Marianne, who had just come in.

'Hmm, is it possible that you kids forgot the hardener?' Piet eyed the spot warily.

'No way? Lena, didn't I tell you that you have to mix it first?' Maxl snapped at Lena.

'And then you rushed off. Had to show Andrew what a big hero you are around here, right?' Martin countered drily. Andrew heard his name and looked from one to the other questioningly.

'Just another example, women and technology,' Stefan butted in with a smirk.

'Oh yeah? And who was it again who spent a solid half hour yesterday trying to pull the main pins out without removing the safeties first?' Marianne hit back, annoyed. Stefan blushed and didn't say another word.

'You said you knew what you were doing, remember, kid? People should give you a bit more credit, right?' Maxl flared up at Martin. Lena was incredibly embarrassed. She hadn't listened. Again. She was thankful to Martin for the way he had defended her, but it was still really unpleasant, especially in front of Maxl. Piet was sure to be disappointed in her again too. He just grinned though.

'Come on, stop arguing. You'll all laugh; exactly the same thing happened to me once. My workshop supervisor had a fit. We can fix it up. Practice makes perfect. Oh, and Martin, have a look in the box by the way, the instructions are still in there.'

Martin pulled the slip of paper out of the packaging and read aloud:

'*If you don't around on the total of the packaging to using, that we believe, we will be able, the whole time, that the mixture is dying…*' He couldn't go any further because he was choking with laughter. 'What's that then?'

'Great isn't it – terrific translation there by the manufacturers. After reading that, you're an instant expert,' grinned Piet. 'So, and now we can wash this dog's breakfast off and start again from the beginning. Stefan you can stay here too for now, and no more quips.' Maxl tried to explain to Andrew what had happened, but his English wasn't quite up to it.

'If your translation just now was as good as the one in the box, well good luck with that!' laughed Marianne. Maxl turned red and went outside with Andrew, looking irritated.

'He could at least help,' grumbled Martin. 'It's his fault after all.'

'That's enough! When everyone's messed up, blaming each other doesn't help. You have to talk to each other BEFORE things go wrong,' Piet resolutely ended the discussion and they set to work. Lena awkwardly studied the toes of her shoes again.

Marianne was watching her.

'Don't take it so much to heart. Like Piet said, it happened to him once too. See, you have to mix the resin and hardener together like this.' Lena was glad to have something to do and took very careful note this time. How humiliating!

24. Autumn in the Workshop

The next few weeks were distinctly calmer. The weather stayed cold, and it often rained on the weekends. The gliding season was effectively over. Piet gave out the dates for the theory lessons and posted a calendar showing when to turn up for duty in the workshop. There was plenty to do over the winter.

At school too, it was clear that the holidays were definitely over. No more off-season. It wasn't only the exacting Frau Böhmer demanding a lot from them now. Somehow or other, all the teachers always seemed to manage to make the work pile up.

'It's unbelievable,' groaned Philipp in the long break at school one day. 'Why do they always set the presentations right in the week when we've already got three projects to write up? And of course I've got football training too, for the game on the weekend.' he sighed theatrically.

Martin nodded gloomily. As usual, Lena had her nose buried in a book.

'What's that you're reading?' asked Philipp. She held up the book but didn't let herself be interrupted. 'Navigation for Beginners,' he read. 'Phew, listen, don't we already have enough to learn? Is it exciting?'

'Mmmm,' Lena didn't really answer. She munched on her sandwich while she read.

'She's determined to cram her way through the entire theory in one season,' said Martin, answering for her. 'She's afraid of falling behind 'cos she's only allowed to go to theory classes every second Saturday.'

'Easy for you to say,' now Lena did look up from her book. 'You've got a season behind you and you already know most of it. The exam in February will be no problem for you.'

'You must be mad! Do you *have* to take the exam in February?' asked Philipp with a frown. It was a mystery to him why anybody would take on such a lot of stress voluntarily.

'Hardly!' answered Martin on her behalf again, sounding a bit resentful. 'It doesn't matter at all! She can't get her licence next year anyway. You have to be sixteen, so she's got at least a year and a half yet.'

'But you promised!' Lena looked at Martin imploringly.

'Yeah, I promised. I'll let you know exactly what we covered, so you don't miss anything, crazy girl,' he answered, shaking his head in disbelief. She just shrugged her shoulders.

'So why can you only go to theory every second Saturday?' Philipp was still struggling to understand why she was so ambitious all of a sudden. This was a side of her that he hadn't seen before. She wasn't usually like this at school.

'The last few tests in German, Maths and French didn't go too well, in fact they went pretty badly,' Lena blushed a little. She was well aware of the reason. It had tousled red hair and freckles. Until now, she had never had problems at school. 'Now I'm only allowed to spend one day per weekend at the airfield. I'm supposed to study. I've got to work in the workshop too, otherwise it costs more. That means workshop one week, theory the next.'

'And are you still working with your mother as well?'

'These days even that's only now and then. I think my mother is really annoyed. As long as things went OK at school there was no problem about the airfield. I actually wanted to earn something towards the cost and help in the shop too, but somehow I can't seem to manage everything.'

Lena kicked a small stone in frustration.

'So, just take it a bit slower, no one's pushing you on the theory and there's no real hurry.' Philipp looked at her uncomprehendingly.

Yet again, it was Martin who spoke first.

'You want to be better than Maxl, don't you? He's the only one in our club who's got through both the theory and the radio endorsement at once, in one winter. But what's the good of that? The radio test isn't till spring anyway. All that effort just because of the gel coat thing?'

'What's it got to do with you?' Lena snarled at him. She grabbed her things and left the boys to themselves.

'Bingo. Looks like you've hit the nail on the head there, doesn't it?' Philipp whistled through his teeth. 'What's going on between her and this Maxl anyway?'

'How would I know, who understands girls?' Martin rolled his eyes.

'And what's with the gel coat story?' Philipp persisted. He had clearly been paying attention.

'You're really interested, aren't you?' Martin eyed his friend searchingly. The bell rang. As they made their way to the classroom, Martin gave Philipp all the airfield gossip. Now he was in his element again!

Lena hadn't heard much of Maxl in the last few weeks. He haunted her thoughts and dreams more or less constantly, but by now the saga of the kiss was so long ago that it almost seemed unreal to her. There were rumours that he had a new girlfriend, but

Lena hadn't seen any evidence of that herself. When they did happen to meet, in the corridor at school or in the workshop on the airfield, they both acted neutrally-friendly, more restrained than anything else. Not that it happened often. Lena was actually rather relieved by that. She had long since given back his iPod. She didn't want to listen to his music anymore.

The whole story had wounded her pride a little. Her motivation and ambition to ace the aviation theory exam knew no bounds. To her amazement, she often met Bolle in the navigation classes.

'What are *you* doing here, haven't you finished your exam ages ago?' she asked him one time.

Bolle ran his fingers through his hair awkwardly. With the amount of gel he used, Lena secretly wondered if his hand might stick.

'Failed Nav, it just won't go into my brain,' he admitted.

'I study with Martin. I can't get my head around it either, but he really gets everything – maybe we could all work together on it sometime?' Lena suggested.

'Great idea, let's do that,' Bolle was pleased. 'Do you have to leave straight after the class today or will you help us in the workshop? Marianne's here too.'

'I've got time, my mother's not coming to pick me up till seven, but tomorrow I'm not allowed out, homework…' Lena made a face.

'I know…I mean, my parents were ridiculously strict at first too. They totally panicked. Thought I'd just throw school away because of flying. As if you were crazy or something.'

'Exactly! You said it,' Lena was relieved that it was the same for other people. 'What are we doing in the workshop today?' she asked him.

'We're onto the 21. Inspecting cracks in the leading edges, root ribs and the entire wings. Depending on what we find, maybe sanding off gel coat and putting more on. Tyre pressure, checking the electrics, whatever crops up you know.'

'Uh oh, gel coat – that sounds familiar. I've had some great experience with that recently,' Lena groaned.

'Don't worry, now that you know how, it's actually really simple. We can do it together anyway, it'll be fun.'

And that's how it worked out too. After the theory class, they met Marianne in the workshop and the three of them got the ASK21 out of the hangar. In the workshop the radio droned away and a blower heater stopped their fingers from freezing off. They got stuck into the work. After a while, Lena found it really comfortable and homely. No one to make stupid remarks, know better about everything or show off. She hadn't felt this good in ages.

They found some surface cracks in the gel coat on one wing, although the fibreglass underneath wasn't damaged. That meant they had to carefully sand off some of the old gel coat around the cracks, then apply some new gel coat. After it had hardened, more sanding and polishing. They did everything in a calm and relaxed atmosphere: they joked around, drank cocoa now and then and enjoyed themselves despite the work.

'Can I ask you a personal question?' Bolle asked, as Marianne was away for a moment. 'Well actually two things.'

'OK, shoot,' Lena was curious.

Bolle took a deep breath.

'Have you heard from Kim lately? Has she said anything about me?'

'Not really,' admitted Lena sadly. 'We write now and then, but we don't actually talk on the phone anymore. We never seem to catch each other. But, well, she's got heaps of new friends now and somehow it just doesn't seem to fit anymore. We seem to have really drifted apart since summer.'

'Hmm, sounds about right, somehow I got the same impression. Only she doesn't write back to me at all anymore.'

'I'm sorry to hear that,' sighed Lena. What else could she say? She was disappointed herself.

'And what happened between you and Maxl?' Bolle continued probing. Just then, Marianne came back in.

Lena bit at her lower lip for a moment uneasily before she answered.

'Actually – nothing, I was just too dumb to realise that he only wanted to have a bit of fun.'

They both stood around awkwardly for a moment with no idea what to say.

'You should see your faces,' grinned Marianne, 'as if someone had just eaten your last piece of chocolate, both of you. Come on, give me a hand to push our darling back into the hangar!' Bolle stuck his tongue out at her, but he had to laugh again. Lena felt much the same. She grabbed the wing tip to steer.

'Forwards!' she commanded, feeling relieved. Finally someone in a similar situation who understands my problems, she thought.

After that Lena tried to be a bit more relaxed about cramming theory.

Her marks at school didn't recover quite as quickly as her mood, although her mother did see some improvement and wasn't as strict about Lena visiting the airfield anymore. Lena helped more often in the bookshop again too.

The cold and snow of winter came rather early this year. Soon afterwards the heating system at the airfield gave up the ghost. For weeks the clubhouse and workshop were both ice cold. Theory lessons and workshop duty had to be cancelled until it could be repaired.

In December, Lena's whole family was laid low with the flu. Jakob got it first and progressively infected everyone else. The flu stretched out till Christmas; a huge success. They tried to make the best of things with the help of fruit punch and cinnamon Christmas cookies. Grandma Liesl was the only one not to catch the infection and she doted on them all devotedly.

By New Year's Eve they were all fit and healthy again and could enjoy the celebrations. Just before midnight, it was traditional to melt lead over a candle and pour it into water. It was fun trying to work out what the resulting shapes meant. When it was Lena's turn, Barbara, Johannes and Jakob all agreed: It was an aircraft wing, and it meant that things would get better for Lena soon. Lena sighed hopefully: wouldn't that be nice!

On New Year's Day, Piet had a surprise for the young trainees. They could each have an hour's flight in the motor glider with him. It was a sunny, ice cold, clear winter's day and everything was covered with a lovely layer of snow like a kitsch Christmas card.

'How different everything looks from up here in winter,' Lena remarked happily after they took off. In the motor glider they sat side by side. As soon as they had reached a suitable height, Piet handed over control.

'You fly it just like a glider; I'll look after all the motor stuff. So, Lena, where do you want to fly?'

'Could we go to Holzhausen? I'd really like to see our house from the air!' answered Lena like a shot.

'Well then, you have control,' laughed Piet. 'Can you find it from up here?'

'I'll just follow the road,' Lena decided.

'Exactly – seek out the landmarks you know. Here's an ICAO map, you've used them in your Nav' classes. I won't say anything.' Piet leaned back and relaxed.

Lena compared the road alignment to the map and sure enough, after ten minutes she could make out Holzhausen. There was the church, the football ground... and there! There was Wiesenstrasse and her house!

'Can we circle here a bit?' she asked imploringly. That's where I live.' She pointed to her house. Piet nodded.

'Of course, but maintain height! We shouldn't go any lower or there'll be complaints about the noise.' Lena flew a few circles. Soon she could even see first Jakob and then her mother rush out of the house into the garden waving enthusiastically.

'Cool,' she cried excitedly.

'OK, that's enough circling, or your neighbours might get uptight. Now imagine you're in a glider and can't find a thermal. Where would you outland?' Lena flew straight and level again. She considered the question.

'Over there behind the sports ground is a huge field. There are never cows or sheep on it and there's no fence.'

'Very good, now show me how,' and so saying, Piet throttled back. The propeller just ticked over and the motor glider lost height rapidly.

'Aha, and what about the noise?' Lena protested half-heartedly.

'This is emergency landing training, I can justify that,' Piet grinned. 'You're pretty much on downwind now; fly the circuit as if you had to land there. Keep a good lookout. Your altimeter reading is no use here; the terrain is lower than the airfield. Keep the aiming point in sight and estimate how far out you should fly.'

Lena concentrated hard on planning her approach and landing and her cheeks glowed red. She carefully kept the aiming point in view the whole time. Just before they would have touched down, Piet pushed the throttle open and they climbed away.

'Very good,' he praised her. 'We'll do that a few more times on the way home.'

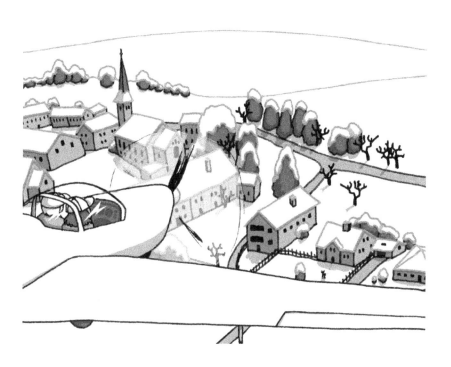

25. Running Errands

After that heavenly day, the airfield seemed to Lena to sink back into deep hibernation – nothing happening at all! Their work in the workshop was as good as done. The weather was bad and really cold. The gliding season wouldn't start for a few weeks yet. Only the theory classes offered any relief from the boredom. However ambitious Lena may have been when theory lessons started last year, she had now decided not to sit the exam in February, so her drive had finally evaporated. Her flight in the motor glider had helped her make peace with herself. What had Martin said after his call with Piet that time? When you fall off a horse, you have to get straight back on. That had been about Martin's crash landing.

Lena's hangar flight last season wouldn't have turned out much better than Martin's experience if it hadn't been for Piet, but unlike Martin, she had never had the chance to get back into the saddle. She had somehow tried to make up for that with especially diligent study.

As soon as Lena had gotten her hands back on the controls and seen that it did actually go quite well, everything was right with the world and she felt good again. The whole time she was flying she didn't think about Maxl, even once. Finally! She felt liberated and elated.

Martin passed his theory exam in February, as everyone had expected. Bolle successfully managed the navigation exam the second time around too. Lena was a little envious of Martin; she would have really liked to have it behind her as well.

Lately, Martin had been helping her more with maths for school than air law or meteorology at the airfield. Lena felt that was more important for the time being. Otherwise, if her marks weren't good enough, she was afraid her mother would put harsh restrictions on her time at the airfield again. At the moment though, Barbara really couldn't complain. Lena was coming to help in the bookshop more often and was now quite good at it. She mostly did her work without Barbara having to tell her what to do.

'Lena! Can you come here please?' called Barbara from the bookshop storeroom.

'What's up?' Lena was in the yard cutting up old cartons to put in the paper recycling. She was wrapped up tightly against the cold and had bright red cheeks from working outside.

'I don't want to shout like this, can you come in please?' came the muffled reply from the storeroom.

'I still need a while here. What is it?' Lena called back. She grinned. She knew precisely why her mother, the walking chilblain, didn't want to come out. 'And anyway it was YOU who started shouting. Come out! It's the start of April already, it's spring.' Barbara appeared in the doorway, shivering.

'Some spring – everything still freezes at night. Bitterly cold. Brrr, that's what I call icy,' she complained. 'Lena, I've got something here to deliver again. Do you want to do it?'

'Hmmm,' muttered Lena, not feeling very motivated. These deliveries came up all the time. It wasn't just dropping off a package. You had to have a friendly chat with the old ladies and smile the whole time – she really didn't feel like it.

'You'd have to go to the retirement home in Waldallee. I think there's a bus that goes to Holzhausen from there, so you can knock off when you're done and take the bus straight home.'

Lena hesitated.

'Oh come on.' Barbara didn't give up.

Lena sighed. Her mother just wasn't going to leave her in peace.

'OK OK, good, I'll do it. Who do I have to deliver the package to?' she enquired in surrender. Barbara's teeth had now actually started chattering.

'Come inside, I'll show you, we can cut this stuff up some other day,' her mother beseeched her, pointing to the pile of empty cartons. Lena kicked the cardboard box that she was still holding in her hand. It went up in a high arc and landed in the bin.

'Goal!' she murmured to herself as she followed her mother inside. Philipp would have been thrilled.

'A Frau Hartmann placed the order. Actually it's a bit strange, I could swear she bought the exact same books from us once before, a couple of months ago.' Barbara trailed behind her on the way back into the shop.

'That is strange, maybe she's buying them as a present for somebody?' Lena speculated. Barbara shrugged her shoulders.

'No idea, I didn't take the order or I would've asked. She hasn't given a direct line number either. If it turns out the order was a mistake, take the books home and I'll reverse it on Monday.'

'OK: retirement home, Waldallee, Frau Hartmann – I'll find her and solve the MYSTERY,' Lena mocked good-naturedly and set off with the books. Actually she was quite glad to be setting off now. She'd get home a bit earlier than normal. As always, she studied the sky on the way. Hopefully the weather would improve soon. It had rained much too often lately and the ground on the airfield was too soft for landing on the grass. It couldn't be long now though. The ASK23 had to be delivered sometime soon for sure and the airfield open day was coming up too, if the weather was good enough. The eternal waiting was getting on her nerves again.

When she got to the retirement home, Lena enquired after Frau Hartmann and was directed to the second floor, room 23. Lena knocked. The door opened and a friendly, elegantly dressed lady asked her in. As Lena had already known, small talk was on the menu… Smile. A moment later her smile froze on her face. Inside, to Lena's intense astonishment, at a small round table, with a carefully laid out tea tray in front of her, sat… Isabella! Isabella looked up at the same moment and almost dropped the sugar bowl in shock. She blushed bright red and glared fiercely at Lena.

'What are YOU doing here?'

'I um… I've got… something to deliver,' Lena stuttered. What was the problem that this cow always had with her?

'Oh, you know each other? How nice! Are you in the same class? I want to know all the details. You really must stay for a cup of tea, young lady.' Frau Hartmann was obviously pleased to have company and quickly fetched an extra cup and saucer for Lena. Isabella's unfriendly stare seemed to quite escape her notice.

'You really don't need to go to any trouble on my account, I have to go anyway…' Lena began, but Frau Hartmann didn't even let her finish.

'Poppycock,' she countered merrily. 'How often does an old biddy like me get a visit from two such nice young ladies at once? Shame on you Bella, that you've never told me about your friend before!'

'We're not… ah whatever.' Isabella stared into her cup sullenly. Lena felt awkward and remained silent. Frau Hartmann poured tea for her.

'There you go, and please help yourself to biscuits,' she prompted Lena. 'Ah, my books,' the old lady opened the package, looking pleased.

'Oh Granny! Not again!' Isabella examined the books with a frown as they emerged.

'Why do you say that?' Frau Hartmann looked from one to the other, bemused.

'You've already bought those books twice before, don't you remember? The last time we even went to the bookshop together.'

'Oh! Are you sure?'

'Yes.' Isabella sighed. Now she looked at Lena with an apologetic expression.

'Could you maybe take the books with you again and exchange them or something?' Lena was surprised to see how sad Isabella looked.

'Of course,' she hurried to say. 'My mother did think something might not be right, would you like some other books instead?'

Isabella sighed dejectedly.

'Actually, it makes no difference. She just likes to shop. Even if she reads the books five times, she still can't remember them.'

'Well I'm allowed to forget things now and then at my age, aren't I? But now girls, tell me something nice!' Frau Hartmann slid around restlessly on her chair.

'Well, you were right, we are in the same class,' Lena began feebly.

'Lena's learning to fly gliders, over in Moorbach, at the airfield,' Isabella suddenly announced loudly, with a look of animosity towards Lena.

'Oh, how wonderful,' her grandmother gushed delightedly, 'but isn't it dangerous?' The enthusiastic expression had vanished now, making way for worry lines on the brow.

'There you have it. You have to understand that everyone in my family believes all pilots have suicidal tendencies and are constantly putting themselves in extreme danger.' Isabella burst out in irritation.

'Yes child, but that's no reason to raise your voice!' Frau Hartmann shook her head disapprovingly.

How did I get into this? Lena wondered to herself. How was she going to get out again?

'Well, learning to fly does carry a lot of responsibility,' she began hesitantly, 'but the training is actually very thorough and it takes quite a long time. Everyone always looks out for each other, you're not alone…' She was struggling for words.

'Have you got any idea how much I envy you?' Isabella suddenly gave her a candid look.

'What, me? Really? Why?' Lena asked, astounded.

'Because you're allowed to fly, of course.' Isabella's face took on a soft, dreamy expression.

'I didn't think you were interested. Why don't you just come to the airfield sometime then?' This was incredible! Isabella, of all people…

'My mother has a profound fear of flying. I'm not allowed. She breaks out in a sweat if she even goes anywhere near an airfield.' Isabella hung her head sadly.

'No way! Isn't there anything you can do?'

'What could I do? She rejects it out of hand and no one's going to force her, why should they?'

'Hmm… have to find some other reason to entice her onto the airfield and then just… hmmmm.' Lena ruminated. There had to be a solution! 'But you do really want to learn to fly?' she probed.

'Totally!' Isabella beamed at her. She hadn't smiled at Lena in ages.

Frau Hartmann had stood up and was clearing the table. Lena got up too.

'Ok. I can't promise anything, I'll have to talk to a few people, but I might have an idea. Does your mother still organise that project day at school at the end of the month?'

'As far as I know,' Isabella looked at her hopefully. 'What are you planning?'

Lena grinned.

'Like I said, I'll have to work a few things out first. See you on Monday?'

'Yep 'course.' Isabella handed her the books looking hopeful.

'OK, see you then. Goodbye, Frau Hartmann. I'll ask my mother if she can't recommend something else for you to read.' Lena left the retirement home feeling excited. She had a terrific idea and it just had to work.

26. Preparations

'I don't know if everything's going to work out the way you imagine it, Lena. If she's scared and doesn't want to fly, I won't be able to do anything about it. And what if, in the end, it's worse than before? You've really taken something on here.' Piet scratched his head thoughtfully. Lena and Martin had cornered him outside the clubhouse on Sunday morning. Even in the car on the way there, Martin had been really enthusiastic about Lena's idea.

'Oh pleaaaaase, please, please! I'm sure you'll be perfect. I asked my dad, but he can't, except on the open day, he'll be right behind you there. Just put on a classy shirt and um… maybe leave out the bucket hat,' Lena grinned encouragingly. Martin was sitting on the rail next to her. He nodded enthusiastically.

'Even if she doesn't take you up on it, you'll improve our marks for dedication and commitment by 1,000 per cent with Böhmer. That can't hurt at all.'

Marianne, who had been following everything, gave a little laugh.

'How can you say no to so much youthful enthusiasm? C'mon Piet, give it a go!'

'OK, I'll do it.' Piet wheezed resignedly. 'When do I have to be there?'

'The Thursday after next, I'll let you know the time. You're the best.' Lena flung her arms around the old instructor's neck jubilantly.

'Yeah well, don't celebrate too soon, you might not be so happy later if I blow it,' Piet countered sheepishly. The whole affair wasn't to his liking at all, but Martin and Lena looked to him so expectantly and trustfully, that he just couldn't refuse. The young people seemed to always imagine that everything was so simple.

'I'll be there. Have you got enough flyers and gummy bears and key rings and whatever other promotional material we've got? I'll bring the model glider with me.' Now that he had agreed to do it, he might as well be well prepared.

'We've got everything,' Martin declared eagerly. 'We've been planning this project day for quite a while now. We have to present our subjects and give talks and so on – there's still a lot of work to do. At the end there's the major presentation in the school auditorium, reported in the school newspaper etcetera – that's where you come in. Isabella's mother simply won't be able to back out. She won't want to show any weakness. She's been on the school council so long and organises all these events.'

'In that case, let's hope we have good weather for the airfield fete.' He paused. 'I need a coffee.' With these words, Piet left them to their own devices and plodded into the clubhouse.

'I think it's really great that you're going to such lengths to help out a classmate.' Marianne nodded in acknowledgement. 'Shall we print out the voucher in the tower? We can make a stack of them, some for the airfield fete too. People always like to buy things like that as presents, for grandchildren or whoever.'

'Good idea,' Lena and Martin jumped down from the rail excitedly and followed Marianne to the small tower. The airfield fete was the next day after project day at school. Hopefully everything would go well. Now they only had to get Philipp on board. He would definitely be in, they were quite sure of that.

They met him the next morning on the school bus. Isabella was there too and boarded the bus a little uncertainly.

'Cool plan! Count me in, of course. She'll get a big article in the school newspaper.' Philipp grinned broadly. He was obviously very pleased to be included. 'There's finally something going on around here!'

'Hi, can I?' Isabella pointed to the empty seat next to Lena, almost timidly.

'Of course!' Lena quickly lifted her school bag out of the way and beamed at her. 'We've got news!'

'Really? What are you planning?' Isabella looked around at them all eagerly. Lena and the boys explained the plan to her. Isabella remained sceptical, but she did manage to summon up a little hope, 'Wow, you're all really working at this! Can I do anything to help?'

'Yep... you can... not breathe a single word of this at home! We have to take her completely unawares and you have to make sure that she doesn't make any plans for the first of May,' declared Lena excitedly. Isabella thought about that.

'I'll manage that somehow and even if this doesn't work out, at least we will have tried.' The bus pulled up outside the school and they all went inside babbling loudly in a jovial mood.

They still had some things to prepare for the so-called project day. Every student had to choose a hobby or a particular subject and give a presentation on it, either alone or in a group. They had to give a talk about what was so special about their chosen subject, explain the details, outline the procedures and processes, prepare posters and brochures, identify their target audience – no limits were put on their imagination. The written articles would be marked, of course. Finally, they would present their projects to their parents and the whole school in the school auditorium. The same day there were performances where others could help. These were usually dance groups, bands or similar types of performance art.

In the last few years, Lena had mostly stayed in the background along with Kim. They had presented a lonely literature café, which most of the other students seemed to find pretty boring.

For Martin and Lena, the choice of subject this year was obvious: gliding. If they had been able to, they would have preferred to just take their classmates to the airfield, but of course that was too much for Frau Böhmer. She had agreed though, to a presentation with pictures on a large screen, with commentary and explanation by an old, experienced flying instructor.

As president of the school council, Frau Peters, Isabella's mother, had been attending these project days for years with the utmost dedication. She organised tables and benches for the auditorium, a fantastic buffet and drinks. She helped wherever she was needed or anything went wrong – missing cables, lighting breakdowns or problems with other equipment.

A day before the event, Lena and Martin talked to Frau Böhmer and suggested a way to acknowledge Frau Peters' dedication. When they mentioned giving her a joy flight, the stern teacher looked up at them in surprise.

'That's a brilliant idea, but is it really that simple? And how much would it cost? To tell the truth, we've been trying to think of a way to thank her for a long time in the faculty – she really does an unbelievable amount. None of us ever would have thought of THAT though.'

'The flight would be free,' Lena explained, beaming. 'The club is pleased that we're trying to attract new members here at school and is happy to treat Frau Peters. We've already arranged everything; she can come straight to the airfield fete the next day. And the school newspaper would like to publish a report about it. Don't you think she'll be delighted?' Lena asked, trying to look innocent. Martin nodded enthusiastically in agreement.

'But that's just wonderful! Lena, Martin, I'm glad to see you both making such an effort. It's really thoughtful of you, I'll discuss this with the Principal right away.'

'But please don't let Frau Peters hear anything about it beforehand, it's supposed to be a surprise,' Lena called after Frau Böhmer, who was already hurrying off to the teachers' common room.

Martin didn't believe his eyes when Frau Böhmer turned around, gave them a conspiratorial wink and said:

'On my honour!'

'Wow, Lena, that was taking sucking-up to a higher level. We'd never have earned that many Brownie points from that dragon any other way in years. That was some idea of yours!' he grinned happily.

In the break, Lena and Isabella huddled under the old shade tree in the schoolyard. That had become a common occurrence lately. Lena was delighted not to have to sit around on her own in the breaks anymore.

Martin really was a dear friend, but she had missed having a girl she could really talk to as a best friend, like Kim.

Now, all at once, Isabella was there.

Lena discovered that *Bella* wasn't as conceited and arrogant as she had always imagined at all. On the contrary! In some ways she was just as shy and insecure as Lena, she just never let on.

Suddenly, there was endless material for discussion and that wasn't only down to Isabella's newly kindled interest in gliding!

'How on earth can girls talk so much?' groaned Martin, not for the first time, and slipped away to join Philipp and the other boys again.

Philipp grinned across at them and gave them the thumbs up.

'I'm so excited,' moaned Isabella. 'It's all set for tomorrow. It'll be so cool if it actually works.'

'Piet'll manage it,' Lena reassured her, 'When he's finished talking your mother's ears off, she'll think she invented flight herself. And after Philipp takes her photo for the school newspaper and everything's so official, with applause in the auditorium and all that – she's bound to go along with it.'

Isabella inclined her head thoughtfully and looked at Lena sideways.

'If you say so. I would have loved to have seen Böhmer's face! I'll never believe either of you that she can laugh.'

The bell rang, and the boys went past them on the way to the classroom. Philipp winked at them as he passed.

'Hey, are you still into him?' Lena asked Isabella softly as they followed the boys inside. 'What happened back then anyway? One moment you were together and then suddenly, radio-silence, just not on speaking terms anymore?'

'You know, his heart wasn't in it. Eventually I just got the feeling he actually loved another girl altogether...' Isabella whispered back.

'I know THAT feeling. That's terrible.' Lena shuddered.

'The airfield guy? What's his name again, Max?'

'Yep, Maxl, how did you know that?'

'Oh, a little bird told me...' replied Isabella cryptically.

Lena looked at her questioningly.

'Well, what does it matter? And what did Philipp say? Were you right?' This was riveting!

'Come on Lena – you must know why he suddenly drops everything and takes photos for you, or puts the school newspaper to work for you, or keeps the spot beside him free for you at the start of the school year?' Isabella rolled her eyes.

'NO WAY! You don't mean that!' cried Lena, dumbfounded and stopped in her tracks.

'Shhh! Be quiet! Keep walking!' Isabella tugged at her arm. 'Has the penny finally dropped?' She grinned.

'I don't believe it! I always thought… well, maybe because of Kim. No wonder – you must have really hated me. Are you still angry?' Lena was truly sorry.

'Nonsense! Not anymore. At first, I really couldn't stand seeing you at all, but eventually it wasn't so bad anymore. Hey, have you noticed how much Martin's changed?'

'Whaaaat?' Lena's astonishment knew no bounds. Didn't Martin look just the same as ever?

'Yeah,' Isabella skirted around the issue. 'He's got nowhere near so many zits anymore and, I don't know, don't you think he's got totally cool lately? What's he been doing out there at the airfield?' She literally turned red.

'Bella!' shrieked Lena excitedly. She could hardly restrain herself. She felt like she wanted to explode with laughter – but she wouldn't do that to her friend. They had just arrived in class at that moment.

'Not a word,' hissed Isabella and walked over to her seat.

Lena sat down next to Philipp, still feeling stunned.

She looked at him in profile. He was talking to Martin about something right across the room.

She hardly listened. He had his hair tied back as usual. With his narrow face, strong chin and dark brown eyes, there *was* something about him. Why had she never noticed it before now?

'What's wrong? Have I got spiders on my head?' Philipp interrupted her revelations, grinning facetiously and groping around on his head. Lena snapped out of it.

'Nah! All good, I was miles away.'

She quickly bent over her school bag and got out a couple of books, so he wouldn't see her red face.

Luckily, Frau Böhmer entered the room just then and she didn't have to offer any further explanation.

27. Piet in Top Form

The next morning chaos ruled in the school auditorium. All the students bustled around excitedly in all directions, busy setting up their stands or preparing their backdrops and scenery. Naturally, Frau Peters was there too. She hectically dashed here and there with a flushed complexion, lending a hand wherever she could. Isabella watched the activities with mixed feelings. As far as her own presentations and performance went, she was serenity itself. She was playing cello in a quartet as usual. It was pretty straightforward. The other musicians had just arrived, and the large audience didn't worry her. Her presentations about the history and construction of cellos and the various compositions for stringed instruments and 'The Significance of Cellos Then and Now' had gone well. The teachers almost always gave musical accomplishments an A at these events. She had no reason at all to worry.

There remained the plan regarding her mother. Even if everything ran smoothly today, what if her mother didn't want to go to the airfield tomorrow anyway or just refused to get in the glider – Isabella could hardly force her mother to go along with it. She tugged on her long ponytail nervously.

In the meantime, Martin and Lena had set up their stand as well as they could. A screen, some collages of pictures and explanations, a large rug and some chairs and cushions. Martin's laptop and a projector were perched on top of a somewhat adventurous construction of chairs and tables.

A huge picture of a glider in the Alps was being projected onto the screen. For Piet's lecture, Martin had selected a complete arsenal of appropriate pictures and put them to music. It was a total mystery to Lena how he had contrived to do all that on the computer – but she thought the effect was fantastic. Piles of brochures, gummy bears, and other promotional material were set out and ready. Only Piet was still missing! Frau Peters came by, handing out programs.

'Wow, Lena, this looks wonderful,' she said, but her expression spoke volumes. 'If I have it right, there'll be a lecture here?'

'Yeah, that's right! We've got…' Martin began.

'Yes, yes,' Frau Peters interrupted him abstractedly. 'That's why I've scheduled you here in the break.' She pointed at the program. 'Otherwise there's always music or presentations on stage, you'd be drowned out, that would be a shame – in the break everyone will be wandering around. A few people are bound to come, those who aren't too afraid of the risk. But honestly kids, I can't believe you put yourselves in such danger. Anything could happen. I would never…'

'Woohoo, this looks really slick, and I see you've brought the hardest worker on board with you. Good call! Are we clear for take off?' she was suddenly interrupted. Frau Peters looked around in surprise and instinctively straightened herself up to her full height. Did the gentleman mean her? Lena bit her lip so she wouldn't burst out laughing. Piet had arrived at precisely the right moment. He was wearing clean trousers and a white shirt. A whiff of eau de cologne wafted over to her and she could have sworn he'd had his hair cut. Unbelievable! The old flying instructor had really made an effort and Lena was almost dumbfounded at the transformation.

Anyone who had seen him as he usually was, scuffling over the airfield in misshapen jeans, old shirt and bucket hat, wouldn't have believed it either.

'Frau Peters, allow me to present my flying instructor, Piet Janssen. He's our Chief Flying Instructor, workshop supervisor and most experienced pilot at Moorbach,' Lena introduced him. Martin grinned and elbowed Lena in the ribs – this was even better than her hustling Frau Böhmer.

'Piet, this is Frau Peters, She's the organiser of this project day and the mother of a classmate of ours.'

Isabella's mother offered Piet her hand. He took it in both of his.

'Frau Peters, I wanted to thank you anyway, how nice to be able to meet you straight away. It's really sensational what you're doing for the young people here. The project day's a terrific idea, did you come up with it on your own?' He kept talking as he led the befuddled woman off towards the drink stand. He winked at Lena and Martin over his shoulder briefly, but didn't interrupt the flow of his words.

'I knew it. When Piet gets going there's no stopping him! Haha!' squeaked Lena, delighted. Isabella ran up excitedly.

'And? How's it going?'

Martin grinned.

'If I know Piet, your mother has already downed her first glass of punch and now they're drinking to fraternity!'

'What?' Isabella blurted out, wide-eyed.

'Rubbish, Martin's exaggerating,' Lena placated her with a grin, 'but Piet's giving her the soft soap! He's good at THAT.'

'Ugh, the suspense is killing me! OK, you've got it covered, I'll get going now.' Isabella had to go on stage and the program was beginning.

The auditorium was jam-packed. Apart from the students, many parents had now arrived to watch the proceedings too. Despite the presentations on the stage, Lena and Martin's stand was well attended in the break. Boys in particular, and lots of fathers, showed plenty of interest in the information.

'Now's our time, Piet, can we start?' Martin called excitedly. He started the presentation. A short video demonstrated a winch launch. He turned the music up full to go with it. People turned around and, curious, came closer. Frau Peters positioned herself at the edge of the gathering and followed the proceedings attentively. Isabella stood close behind her and clenched her fists nervously. Piet didn't need a microphone. He greeted the audience cheerfully like a showman, as if he had never done anything else in his life. 'Please stow your tray tables and return your seatbacks to the upright position, Ladies and Gentlemen. Join us for a while in the wonderful world of gliding.' he boomed out over the heads of the audience. The crowd laughed and moved in closer.

Piet briefly and concisely explained the principles of flight and what was required to get a licence. He emphasised the responsibility taken on so young, the teamwork on the airfield, and all the social trappings as well as the technical know-how that would be learnt along the way. Martin showed the corresponding pictures that he had prepared. Piet elegantly demonstrated an aerobatics routine with a model of an ASK21. He deliberately exaggerated the manoeuvres because he knew how silly they could look. The laughs were definitely on his side. Even Frau Peters smirked cheerfully.

Without warning, Maxl had appeared behind Lena.

'Wow, you've organised this brilliantly,' he whispered in her ear, so as not to disturb Piet. 'I would never have thought of it. I presented gliding once, on our project day, two years ago – but this is something else. How did you convince Piet to do it? He's awesome!' Lena grinned a satisfied grin.

'Let me guess, feminine charm, right? I'm really envious.'

'Shh!' Lena didn't want to miss any of the lecture. Maxl was too late now anyway. Isabella grinned at her across the crowd.

It was going really well! There was loud applause for Piet. Martin and Lena were busy handing out brochures and eagerly answering curious questions.

Even Maxl helped. He wanted to share in the sudden success and show that he belonged to the club too.

Then the stage program started up again. Frau Peters congratulated Piet exuberantly on his successful lecture and disappeared into the crowd again.

'I've already got some great photos.' Philipp enthusiastically pushed his way to the stand through the crowd. 'Frau Böhmer will give the closing address later, that will be exciting too. Will you go up Lena, or will Piet do it?'

'Oh, I don't know,' Lena was starting to feel a little uneasy.

'Just go together,' suggested Isabella. 'That'll look best anyway.'

'If you say so,' Lena felt quite weak in the knees.

'You can do it! No sweat! See you later, I have to go.' Phillip headed off with his camera at the ready.

'What are you planning?' asked Maxl.

'Don't be so nosey, young man, you'll see,' Piet laid a reassuring hand on Lena's shoulder. 'So, I've done my bit, now it's your turn.'

After the show ended, Frau Böhmer came on stage. Lena followed Piet to the front with her heart beating fast.

'Good luck!' Isabella crossed her fingers so hard that it actually hurt.

Frau Böhmer thanked the students and the other organisers for their efforts and their dedication and waffled on for a while about the objectives and significance of the event.

'Now!' Isabella followed the proceedings minutely and felt nervously for Martin's hand. He held hers very firmly.

'And finally we've got a very particular thank you, which I'm delighted to say has come from the students – Frau Peters, would you please come up to the stage for a moment? Lena, you too?' Isabella's mother climbed the stairs to the stage looking surprised. Lena and Piet followed her. Lena cleared her throat and took a deep breath.

'Frau Peters, everyone knows how much work you've put into the project days over so many years, so this year we'd like to give you a special treat. Tomorrow is airfield open day at Moorbach airfield and as a particular thank you we would like to present you with a free flight in our two-seater! Your pilot will be Piet.'

Piet handed Frau Peters an envelope to loud applause. Flash! Philipp snapped away diligently. Isabella's mother blushed red and looked wide-eyed.

'Oh! Thank you, but I...,' she floundered helplessly.

Frau Böhmer continued.

'I think it's quite a wonderful token of appreciation for your tireless efforts, Frau Peters. You have earned it! Our school newspaper will be there too of course to record everything – so you'll get some lovely pictures as souvenirs. My thanks to everyone once again and I hope you all have a refreshing and relaxing weekend!'

With that, the event was over.

28. The Airfield Open Day

The next morning, everyone arrived early at the airfield. Everything had to be decorated for the big event. It looked like the weather meant to be kind to them.

'Have you heard from Isabella?' asked Martin, as they pushed the ASK21 to the launch point with Marianne.

'Yeah, we chatted online,' Lena reported excitedly, 'she says her mother was in a total flap yesterday at home, but they're coming. Philipp was really smooth too. He arranged with Frau Peters straight off to get a lift to the airfield with them, so he can cover it for the school paper. She had no excuse, Böhmer was standing right behind them.'

'Well, it sounds like Piet did a good job yesterday,' grinned Marianne.

'He was unbelievable! You should have seen it; he had her wrapped around his little finger. If we'd been on our own, I'll bet the effect wouldn't have been half as good.' Martin weighed down the wing with an old tyre so the 21 wouldn't fly solo while they were setting up everything else. Maxl and Bolle set out chairs and sun umbrellas around the launch point table. They tested the radio contact to the tower and the telephone line to the winch. Stefan blew up balloons and put them up in every possible place, and then some.

'Hey Lena,' Bolle called over to them. 'Did I hear right? You lot stole the show yesterday? I would love to have been there!'

One of Stefan's balloons escaped his lips and flew straight into Martin's face. They had to laugh at his stunned expression.

'Oops, sorry,' mumbled Stefan, with the next balloon already in his mouth.

'So, what's going on? Spill the beans!' Maxl waved Lena and Martin over to him.

'It's like this: a classmate of ours, Isabella, wants to fly, but she's not allowed. Her mother is terrified. So, we planned giving her mother the free flight in a way that she couldn't refuse, with the school paper and all the trappings! Piet was supposed to butter her up and make her feel safe. That worked out brilliantly yesterday, and today we have to make it work just as well. Hopefully she'll see that Bella's in good hands here and let her fly. Will you all help?'

'Great plan!' Bolle was impressed. 'Is she cute?'

'The mother or the daughter?' smirked Martin.

'Oh, please!' Marianne looked at them sternly over the top of her sunglasses.

'You bet,' grinned Maxl. 'We're in, right?'

'You can count on me. When are they coming?' asked Bolle.

'About eleven, I think. We should get some barrier tape and peg out the launch point, otherwise people will be running right across it. I'll just drive down to the workshop and get some, we've run out here.'

'I'll come with you!' Maxl jumped into the Lepo beside her.

Lena drove off. It was the first time since the kiss that they had really been alone. Just don't get nervous now, she thought to herself, in high spirits. Two nights ago she had talked to Bella for hours on the phone. They had been so flustered about the project day, but of course they had talked about boys too. Lena had related the entire story about Maxl to Bella. Like a real best friend, she hadn't laughed at Lena or thought she was dumb or naive. On the contrary, she had advised her to take the guy to task and spell everything out clearly, once and for all.

'So? Everything OK?' Lena looked at him briefly sideways. Attack was the best form of defence, Bella had said. She didn't plan to stand before him stuttering like a little first-year with flushed cheeks again. Those days were over! Maxl grinned, amused.

'You're in a good mood today! How come?'

'I'm really looking forward to Bella and Philipp coming later; it'll be cool, it's just got to work with Bella's mother.'

'Philipp, I see, that's the football dude with the camera, right?'

'Yeah, got a problem with that?' Lena answered levelly.
Maxl lifted his hands defensively.

'What gives you that idea? I was only asking.' For a moment neither said anything. 'Lena, what I still wanted to ask you, about that time…'

'Yes?' Lena made herself look busy and swerved to avoid a pothole.

'Well,' Maxl dithered. 'I wasn't sure how you'd taken it. You were so quiet in winter. I just wanted to know if everything's all right between us?'

'Well, at least you came straight to the point!' Lena returned snidely. 'Imagine if I'd been struggling with it for, oh I don't know, months or something.' She stepped on the brakes, stopped the car, took a deep breath and looked at him. Then she had to grin. Actually – it didn't hurt anymore!

'I was furious with you. There it is. But now it just doesn't matter. Seriously.'

It was as if someone had suddenly lifted a huge weight off her shoulders. She had said it. Finally! It hadn't even been bad. Why hadn't she done it much earlier?

'I'm sorry. Honestly. I've been wanting to give you this back the whole time – maybe it'll bring us luck today?' Maxl really did look miserable. In his hand he held Lena's lucky armband, from Jakob.

'Well then, nothing can go wrong now, thanks,' said Lena happily. 'And now you can let me in on one secret. Are you together with that girl you were smooching with in the café that time? Just for curiosity's sake.'

'Nah. She's going out with a guy from her class, a total idiot. Now you know.' Maxl sighed gloomily.

Lena made an effort to keep a straight face.

'So, now everything's out in the open,' she grinned and drove on. She parked the Lepo in front of the workshop.

Two hours later, Piet officially opened the fete with a short speech. A great many visitors had found their way to the airfield and were sauntering around the antique aeroplanes outside the festively decorated hangar.

Joy flights were on offer in the motor gliders, the old Cessna and, of course, in the glider.

The program kicked off with an old biplane giving an aerobatics display. Loud music rang out over the airfield. People tilted their heads back and looked into the sky with rapt attention. The sausage stand was well attended too and next to it was a café stall with coffee and cake. Marianne organised a paper plane competition for the smaller children, where there was a glider flight to be won every hour.

Lena and Martin sat on the barrier at the edge of the runway, waiting to transport guests to the launch point with the bus. A couple of the older licenced pilots would fly the passenger flights. Maxl wasn't allowed yet. He hadn't yet flown enough hours since his exam. Bolle was sitting in the winch cab, feeling bored and Maxl retrieved the cables with the Lepo. If no guests came, they would at least do a couple of display launches in the single seaters to attract people's attention.

After a while the first paper plane winners came over to them. It was already nearly 11 o'clock.

'Martin, would you take them to the launch point? I want to wait here for Bella,' Lena asked.

'Sure, we've got so many helpers today, they don't need us at the launch point. I'll be back in ten minutes.' A winning family with two children climbed into the old bus and Martin drove them cheerfully to the launch point.

He had scarcely disappeared around the corner when Philipp, Isabella and her mother promptly turned up. Frau Peters was pursing her lips in a tense expression. Even at a distance, Isabella threw Lena imploring looks. Philipp was obviously the only one in a good mood, swinging his camera happily.

'Frau Peters! Over here!' Lena waved them over. Just then, Paul, her father, taxied up and stopped behind her in the Cessna. An older couple climbed out and thanked him profusely for a wonderful flight.

'Dad! Can you come here for a moment please?' Lena winked at him meaningfully.

'Just a moment,' Paul finished saying goodbye to his guests and leapt casually over the barrier.

'Frau Peters – this is my father. Papa, this is Isabella's mother, she was awarded the joy flight in the ASK21 yesterday.'

'Welcome to the airfield, Frau Peters, you've really hit the jackpot there. But first you'll want to bolster yourself up a bit, won't you? Come along and I'll show you where the best treats are.' Lena's father offered her his arm gallantly. Frau Peters didn't look quite so pasty anymore and the two of them headed off towards the drinks stand.

'Phew!' Isabella let out a huge sigh. 'She's been bleating non-stop since yesterday. I even went as far as persuading her not to do it after all, but then she harped on about how she could hardly snub the school after such a nice gesture etcetera etcetera. – If only she knew.'

'My dad will look after her. Martin's coming back with the launch point bus – Piet's over there to welcome her. Fingers crossed,' Lena consoled her.

'At least you're actually both here. It could have happened that she just stayed home, couldn't it? We'll take care of the rest too, wait and see!'

'Philipp peppered my mother with questions all the way here in the car, supposedly for the article in the school paper. I reckon she didn't get a moment to think. But what questions! How did you come up with all that rubbish?'

'What questions?' repeated Lena looking at Philipp curiously. He had sat in a car with Isabella and her mother and tried his best to make everything work. It might have been for Isabella and the school newspaper article, but Lena couldn't tell. Her heart did whisper that he had done it for her. Philipp's ears turned a little red.

'You know, like whether she believes driving a car's safer than flying or taking a train, what her first ever flight was like, if she's ever controlled a plane, how much she knows about flying, whether many people really have a fear of flying rather than just getting worked up about their own lack of knowledge, what she feels about the proportion of women to men in aviation, what she'd say if Isabella became an astronaut. Just stuff like that.'

Isabella rolled her eyes and laughed.

'Right – but it sounded more like: Frau Peters, which is better, driving a Porsche to a night club at seventeen or flying cross country alone at sixteen? And similar nonsense!'

'And she didn't just let you out at the nearest bus stop? How tolerant!' laughed Lena and poked Philipp in the ribs cheekily. He caught her hand and pressed it briefly, but let it go again quickly as if he had burnt himself on a stovetop. He looked at her searchingly. Lena lowered her head and self-consciously hid her eyes behind a wisp of hair.

'Honestly, I was just waiting for her to pull over,' laughed Isabella.

Martin came back and Paul manoeuvred Frau Peters gently but firmly into the back of the bus.

'Martin and Lena will take you to the launch point, Piet will be there, you've already met him. Good luck, you'll be fine, enjoy your flight!'

Isabella's mother looked out the window unhappily and sighed, much as her daughter had a short while ago.

Lena, Philipp and Isabella quickly jumped in after her and they headed off for the launch point. It had to happen quickly now, before she had a chance to reconsider in the face of so many aircraft.

Isabella sat up the front with Martin.

'You're really good at driving,' she openly admired him. Martin's ears turned red. Lena grinned – hopefully he wouldn't stall the engine when he parked it again, as usual. That'd be the end of that good impression.

On the way, the ASK21 made a gentle, elegant landing beside them on the grass runway, with Fritz and a young girl on board. The girl scrambled out of the glider and whooped for joy.

'Let us out here Martin, we'll give a hand,' called Lena spontaneously. 'Come on, Frau Peters, everyone mucks in on the airfield, we're a big team.'

She was already springing out of the bus. Isabella and Frau Peters followed hesitantly. Philipp pulled out the camera.

'We'll help!' Lena waved to Fritz. When they arrived at the glider she grabbed the wing tip and sent Isabella and Frau Peters to the leading edge beside the fuselage where they could push.

'And now push it backwards please!' Lena directed cheerily. Fritz briefly introduced himself. The young girl, who had just had a flight, rattled away endlessly to him excitedly. As soon as he could get a word in, Fritz tried to make polite conversation with Isabella's mother.

'It seems like the little one is mightily impressed,' Frau Peters replied with a laugh. By the time they were nearly at the launch point, Piet had already spotted Isabella's mother and came up to her with a broad grin.

'Fritz, you have to have a break now, it's Frau Peters' turn. She's the young people's guest of honour.'

'No, please, I wouldn't want you to go out of your way,' said a nervous Frau Peters defensively.

'You're not putting us out at all, and besides, the kids have put in so much effort for you, we don't want to dither around now.'

'Have they really?' She turned around and looked at Lena and Martin in some surprise. Lena pretended to sort out something in the cockpit of the ASK21 busily. Just at that moment, the Lepo arrived with some momentum and came to rest beside Frau Peters. Maxl jumped out. He greeted her exuberantly and then turned to Isabella.

'Bella, can you help me with the cables please?' Isabella followed him to the Lepo and helped him get the cables ready for the next launch.

'I'm so nervous,' she whispered softly.

'I know, Lena told us everything. Piet'll do it. She'll feel as safe with him as she does at home. Here, pull this over to the glider.' He handed her the end of the rope with the ring for hooking on. He drove the Lepo off to the side and walked back to them at the glider.

Meanwhile, Piet had helped Frau Peters put the parachute on and reassured her several times that it was purely a precaution.

'Safety is paramount. We check the glider and all the equipment repeatedly before use. And we don't even have a motor to break down. So, Lena will help you get in…'

Frau Peters clambered into the glider carefully, with wobbly knees. Philipp hurriedly snapped photos. Lena helped her do the harness up and explained the instruments in the cockpit. Quite against her inclination, Isabella's mother was actually impressed at the way Lena did all that as a matter of course. Lena closed the canopy and went to the wingtip.

At that moment, Frau Peters first spotted her daughter standing beside the glider with the cable in her hand and Maxl beside her.

She watched with close interest as the nice, good-looking boy showed her daughter how to hook the cable on to the glider. Then Isabella waved to her briefly and took a few steps back. They were off! Philipp shot lots of photos of the launch and then they could only wait.

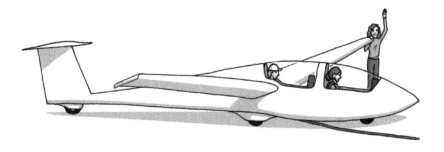

'How long will they stay up?' asked Philipp, looking around at everyone.

'Hmmm, there's a few bubbles already, Piet's sure to find a thermal – the question is whether your mother goes along with it, Isabella,' Martin considered doubtfully.

'Well, at least she didn't scream on the launch, maybe it was all just a bit too sudden,' Isabella grinned. Now that her mother was finally in the air, all the tension dropped away. They really had done everything they could – if *that* wasn't enough, then it just wasn't meant to be.

Lena, on the other hand, gnawed nervously at her knuckles. She *had* organised everything after all. If Frau Peters was sick or had a panic attack in the glider... hopefully everything would go well!

Piet stayed up for a little while in a thermal. In the meantime, other guests had arrived at the launch point for flights, so after fifteen minutes, he brought the ASK21 back in for a gentle landing.

Isabella's mother climbed out of the glider. She swayed a little on her feet, but her face still held a robustly healthy colour. Isabella, Philipp, Lena and Martin were already waiting to push the glider back. Frau Peters thanked Piet, obviously relieved to be back on solid ground. Then she looked energetically around for her daughter.

'So, that was that. Thankfully! Come on my child, we're going home; I've got visitors coming later. Philipp, are you coming?' Lena swallowed, feeling disappointed. This didn't sound good.

'Can't I stay a little longer?' Isabella begged, 'I'd really like to watch some more.'

'Not today. You can see what's going on here; you'd only be in the way. Another time. We'll talk about it at home, all right? Piet explained a few things to me up there...' She obviously didn't want to discuss it any further. She nodded to everyone, turned around and headed off for the car park.

Isabella shrugged her shoulders in resignation.

'Thanks Lena, thanks Piet, I have to go.'

Philipp muttered a curse, 'I'll go with them too, I have to go to training later, ciao.' He said his goodbyes and quickly followed the other two.

Lena and Martin watched them go feeling rather taken aback. That really was a sudden departure.

'What did you tell her?' Lena grilled Piet aggressively as the three of them pushed the glider back.

'The truth of course,' Piet was cool as a cucumber.

'And that is?'

'That her daughter must really seriously want to learn to fly if her friend moves heaven and earth to help make it happen.'

Lena groaned.

'OK, that's that then.' Martin rolled his eyes.

'Calm down, both of you! She was very impressed with how you all pulled together for Isabella. She told me that up till now you weren't really such good friends. Then it was my turn to be surprised, to be honest. She did say the professional supervision here on the airfield was to her liking,' Piet grinned at them. 'You done good. I think she'll talk to Isabella and if her father agrees too, Isabella's bound to be allowed to start here soon.'

Lena jumped for joy. The 21 wing swung perilously, but she didn't let it fall.

'Piet, you're my hero, I knew you could persuade her,' she proclaimed.

'You've got yourself to thank, my dear. We were all only extras. I'm proud of you!' Piet smirked happily. 'By the way, have either of you noticed what's parked over there by the trees behind the new hangar?'

Martin strained to look around.

'Do you mean the glider trailer? What's in it?'

'I'll give you three guesses!'

'The 23! Finally!' rejoiced Martin and Lena with one voice.

'Precisely. And if everything goes well here today, after we've cleaned up tomorrow, we can get on with it. You both flew good launches in the two-seater last week. Tomorrow morning, we'll do a few more, then into the single seater. Martin, you first!'

Lena's heart beat faster at the prospect; Martin went pale. He remembered the K8 landing only too well, but that was history!

29. Spot Landing

It turned out to be a very long day for Lena and all the others. The Open Day was a complete success. Bella even sent a few brief text messages during the day. She and her parents would drop in at the airfield tomorrow to pick up all the information and forms. She was allowed to fly! She'd tell Lena the rest of the story on the phone that night. Lena was overjoyed. Bella, at the airfield, how cool was that!

Paul took her and Martin home in the evening. Lena ran straight to the phone to call Isabella and Paul told her astonished mother and Johannes the whole story.

An hour later, just after Lena had hung up, the phone rang again. It was Philipp.

'Turn on your computer, I just sent you an email,' he prompted her. Lena turned on the PC and exuberantly told him the news while she waited for it to boot up. She opened his mail.

'Cool, the article for the paper. Great pictures, wow! It's just like I imagined it. You're great, thank you!'

Philipp was bashfully modest.

'And? Are you all going flying tomorrow? The weather should stay good.'

'Bella's coming, of course, but she's got to fill out a stack of paperwork and get a medical before she can start learning. And we've got a new glider. Have a guess who's allowed to fly it tomorrow? Martin and me.' Lena was still really happy.

'Wow, congratulations, that's a big deal, right?'

'Wouldn't you like to come to the airfield again? It was a shame that you had to leave so soon today,' Lena blurted out. She blushed. Good thing he couldn't see her, she thought.

Philipp hesitated briefly.

'I can't, unfortunately, we've got a game tomorrow.'

'Of course, silly of me, naturally,' Lena quickly backpedalled, feeling sheepish.

'No. Don't get me wrong. I would really like to see you again tomorrow,' Philipp assured her.

'Really? But I know how it is; you could have asked me to come to your game and I wouldn't have had time either!' She could feel her heart beating.

'Hmmm,' Philipp pretended to deliberate. 'When you look at it that way, we're even.' Lena could literally hear him grinning.

'If there was no gliding, would you come?' he persisted.

Ouch, he'd got her there! Lena had to smile.

'Mayyybe,' she answered, with accentuated vagueness.

'Well then, I'll let you explain that to me in more detail,' Philipp laughed, amused.

They talked on the phone for another two hours. Lena had never felt so close to Philipp before. Some time in the middle, her mother had brought Lena some dinner in her room on a tray, which was unusually accommodating of her.

'One more hour, then lights out. For a change!' whispered Barbara, before quietly leaving the room again.

Sometime or other Philipp told Lena about Kim's emails and how they had come to nothing in the end. He told her about Isabella and how he had disappointed her. There *had* been another girl, but he didn't say anything more about that. He didn't need to.

Lena knew who he meant now. She told him about Maxl and even a little about Martin's advances. Philipp had suspected something of the kind.

'Lena! It's time.' Barbara stuck her head in the door.

'I have to go, my mother…' said Lena reluctantly. Now of all times!

'Ok. See you on Monday. I'll look forward to it,' he said softly. Lena's heart leapt.

'Me too, thanks again for the article.' She hung up.

She was much too excited to sleep and after her mother had said good night, she got up again. She wrote Kim a long email and told her about Isabella, the project day, the airfield fete – and about Philipp. Then she turned off the computer and the light and finally went to bed. Her phone gave a muffled buzz.

'GOOD NIGHT! THINKING OF YOU — P.'

She fell asleep with a satisfied smile on her face.

Lena woke early the next morning. She was wide-awake even though she had slept so little. After a quick breakfast, Martin's mother drove her and Martin to the airfield.

It was calm and still on the airfield this early in the morning. Piet, Marianne, Maxl, Bolle, Stefan and a few others were already there too. With their combined efforts, they cleared away the remains of the open day and eventually got the gliders out. Finally, they rigged the ASK23 that was still in its trailer. Fritz was going to take his time and have a flight in it while the trainees flew circuits with the two-seater. He would take a high aerotow behind the Cessna.

Around midday, Isabella came to the launch point with her parents. The adults greeted one another cordially. Lena and

Isabella huddled together under the ASK21 wing. Martin joined them with the ASK23 flight manual.

'So,' he said to the girls, 'now you can finally tell me why Frau Peters agreed in the end after all. She didn't seem too happy to me after her flight yesterday.'

Isabella grinned.

'She wasn't. She was actually in quite a bad mood. But Piet also told her *why* Lena had started the whole campaign. She was pretty impressed despite herself. She was also impressed with the whole way you all take it for granted that you take responsibility for each other and how everyone knows so much. Martin, you drive a car as if it were the most natural thing in the world, Lena explained the cockpit to her like an old hand. Mama was simply gobsmacked. She had a bit of a guilty conscience on my account too – because she never noticed how important it was to me.' Isabella coloured a little. 'She was really upset about that... Maybe it was my fault too. I should have fought a bit harder for it. But then, luckily, you two showed up. I'm so grateful,' she beamed. She hugged Lena tightly once and, on the spur of the moment, kissed Martin on the nose. Martin's ears turned bright red. Lena grinned happily.

'And? Ready?' she asked him excitedly with a glance at the flight manual. They had been taking turns quizzing each other on the vital points now and then the whole morning.

'I wish I could start today too,' said Isabella dreamily with a gleam in her eye. 'But Piet will take me for a trial flight later. That will be cool.'

'Great,' confirmed Martin, 'You'll have thermals too, it's already looking good. Only it's pretty windy today. Hopefully you won't be sick.'

'You don't give us girls much credit, do you? You were overly concerned on my behalf back then too.' Lena objected with a laugh. Martin blushed. Isabella laughed good-naturedly.

'I expect I'll survive,' she reassured him.

Martin pushed off and got ready to fly the ASK23. Piet kneeled beside the cockpit and went through everything again one last time. Lena listened carefully too. Martin would fly three flights and then it would be her turn.

Martin did well. Lena watched his take-offs and landings intently. In the meantime, Bolle and Maxl had taken Isabella under their collective wing and she was practicing driving the Lepo. Her parents had disappeared to the tower with Marianne to settle the formalities.

Eventually it was Lena's turn. She thought about Philipp briefly. She still hadn't told Isabella anything about their phone call yesterday. She would definitely have to rectify that situation soon.

Everything was suddenly going so quickly! It was a shame he couldn't be here now. Lena took the parachute from Martin. Her heart was pounding. Piet came over.

'So, Lena, we've been through everything once already. It's not very different to the ASK21. The aircraft is smaller of course, so it's lighter. Take care not to fly a kavalierstart or branch off. Keep the transition to the climb phase under control, if you please! I'll be on the radio the whole time.'

Lena climbed into the glider and did up the harness. She closed the canopy. She went through the checklist with complete concentration:

Her harness was good, canopy closed and secure, canopy jettison locked, airbrakes closed and locked, trim set fully forward, altimeter set, radio on, controls – full and free movement, wind from the west, runway clear, emergency options identified – she was ready. She gave Piet a sign and he took up the cable.

'Open!' came the command. Lena pulled the release handle. Piet put the ring on the end of the cable into the open beak of the release. 'Close!' She let go again, the beak closed, and the cable was hooked on.

Isabella and Maxl waved from the launch point table. Martin grinned from a distance and gave her the thumbs up. Piet lifted the wing. Take up slack. All out, all out! Lena followed the winch commands in her mind. She was off!

The last time she had been this excited was her first solo flight. This felt similar. As Piet had said though, it was like ASK21-light. Lena flew a perfect circuit and then another one straight afterwards.

Before the third launch, Piet came over again.

'That went very well. You can thermal a bit this time, like Martin did before. Cloud base is high; you should be able to stay up for an hour easily. But be careful! The wind's picked up. Particularly up high, you'll drift downwind a lot, so keep on your toes and stay in range of the airfield! OK? And have fun!'

Straight after the release, Lena searched out her first thermal. Sure enough, it was going quite high. She didn't climb right up to cloud base; she was afraid of drifting too far downwind. It wasn't so easy to stay close to the airfield without losing too much height.

'Piet, should I land back? I keep getting blown downwind?' she asked over the radio.

'Be a bit more daring, you're staying too low, take one all the way to the top,' he lent her courage. All right then! She struggled on. Sure enough, she got a good 500 metres higher and had enough in reserve to fly back to the airfield, into wind.

Fritz had now taken over the radio at the launch point and was keeping an eye on Lena; Piet was in the motor glider with Isabella. Typical, thought Lena, she got to sweat it out in the thermals and the instructor made it easy for himself with an engine on Bella's first ever flight. She could clearly see Piet and Bella joining the thermal under her now. They had turned off the engine. Cool! She waved to Bella, who gesticulated wildly in reply. The thermals were going even higher now; she was nearly at 1500 metres. She had never been this high before. She couldn't go any higher. Above her was controlled airspace for the big jets and she wasn't allowed to enter it without permission, so time to go back to the airfield again. Piet had flown off in another direction. After all, he did have an engine in case he happened to bomb out.

Lena pointed the nose of the ASK23 towards the airfield and sped up. Phew, it was going down pretty fast now. It hadn't been this bad earlier. The last few times, she had always found a cloud beside the airfield, this time it dispersed with the wind before she got there. There was constant sink. Not a thermal to be found. Would it be enough? Lena doubted it. From this height, she would hardly make it back to the airfield if she couldn't climb in one or two more thermals on the way.

Would she have to land out? Oops! Not that!

'Piiiet? I'm not sure if I'll make it to the airfield,' Lena said nervously on the radio.

'OK, turn around, go back to your last thermal and get some more height again, climb as high as you can. You'll make it there – we'll come over to you!' Lena turned around immediately. After a short while something picked up a wing again and she turned into the same thermal she had been in before with relief. Only she now found herself quite a way further to the east.

She had drifted a fair way with the wind, but she was gaining height again now. Just then she spotted the motor glider.

'You stay here Lena, I'll search for another thermal closer to the airfield and maybe there you can get enough height to make it to the airfield against the wind,' Piet directed.

Lena climbed up almost to the top of the thermal, only leaving some clearance below the cloud. Then she stayed close to the thermal and hung around, topping up height in the thermal from time to time. She may not be losing any height this way, but she was being blown further downwind all the time. She ardently hoped the thermal wouldn't peter out. Piet was back.

'It does actually seem quite bad at the moment, Lena, can you keep going for a while? Everything OK?' asked Piet, concerned.

'Everything's OK so far,' Lena did feel nervous, but apart from that everything was fine.

'Then we'll stay here for a while and I'll fly out towards the airfield now and then and see if any thermals develop.'

That's what they did, but it didn't get better. Piet discussed the situation with Fritz over the radio. Lena listened in of course. Around that time, she noticed that she was now getting quite close to Holzhausen. She really had drifted a long way with the wind. Aside from Piet, no one was speaking on the frequency anymore. Piet had taught her that in an emergency, no one except those involved should talk on the frequency, so that important transmissions wouldn't be blocked. Only one person at a time could talk on the radio, in turns – two or more at the same time just made noise that nobody could understand. Was this an emergency? Lena tightened her grip on the control stick.

'So, Lena, we can't keep going round in circles forever. Do you remember our flight on New Year's Day?'

'Of course!' Lena's heart beat loudly. She was almost certain Piet could hear it.

'Do you think the field behind the sportsground in Holzhausen is still as well mown as you said it was in winter?' asked Piet.

'It looks like it; I went past only last week,' croaked Lena nervously.

'Then fly there,' he decided. 'We're not taking any more risks. There's nothing doing towards Moorbach, the weather's getting worse if anything. No thermals. You won't be able to make it to the airfield, but you've got enough height to get to Holzhausen with the wind and still plan a proper landing. I'll stay behind you off to the side and help! Nothing to worry about, we'll have plenty of time to prepare.' He sounded quite calm.

How does he do that, Lena asked herself. She acknowledged his instructions on the radio and headed for Holzhausen. Her heart was in her throat, but she was concentrating so much that she hardly noticed. There was the Holzhausen church – and right behind it the sportsground. There was even a football match on. There was the field she was supposed to land on; it looked clear.

'Well done Lena, can you see your field?' asked Piet.

'Yes, over behind the sportsground, looks clear,' confirmed Lena.

'Very good, you've got enough height to hang around here and have a good look at everything. You can lose another two hundred metres yet, otherwise you'll be too high on final to get down on the field and you'll fly right over it and end up in the car park. Everything has to be just right now; there's not as much space here as on the airfield! You're landing to the west again, so pick yourself an aiming point abeam the road, can you see that?'

'Yes, got it!'

'Then imagine you're now in the circuit joining area just like at the airfield. When you're 150 metres lower, enter downwind and fly the circuit and landing the same as always. I'll stay with you and climb away when you're down safely – OK?'

Lena swallowed.

'Yep, OK!' She did everything just as he had said. Out of the corner of her eye, she could see that he stayed behind her and off to one side, following all her movements.

'Straighten up there and join downwind! You're doing great.' Lena levelled out. She felt as if she had never flown another aircraft. She controlled her angle to the aiming point without thinking about it, almost as a matter of course.

No one was moving on the sports ground now. Everyone was spellbound by the two aircraft, circling ever lower overhead.

'Turn base, unlock the airbrakes!' directed Piet. Lena turned 90 degrees to the left, onto the base leg. Estimating the angle again, Lena thought it looked steep. She opened the airbrakes a little.

'Airbr... – you're already onto it, great, keep that up,' Piet praised her.

'Final, half brakes!' Lena turned onto the final approach and opened the airbrakes about halfway. The field was now right in front of her. To the left of it was the sportsground. She could imagine Piet behind her on her right, but she couldn't see him.

All her concentration was now directed at her aiming point on the field, abeam the sportsground access road. It was hard to believe she had happily strolled past only a few days ago.

'Carefully put the brakes away just a little, just like that. Hold your speed, don't get any slower, you're doing great!' Lena was now directly over the field. 'Start the flare now!'

Lena followed Piet's instruction automatically, but sometimes she had already begun to act before he said anything. She carefully pulled back on the stick and moved her gaze from the aiming point to the horizon at the far end of the field. The glider rumbled when she landed on the field. She pulled the airbrakes all the way out now to operate the wheel brake. The 23 rapidly slowed to a standstill. For a moment the wings stayed poised horizontally in the air, then the left wingtip slowly lowered itself to the ground. She heard the motor glider power on and climb away overhead.

'Fantastic! Very well done! Great! We'll fly home and get the trailer. Hang in there,' rejoiced Piet. She could hear Bella cheering in the background.

She had done it! She had landed out. Even Maxl hadn't done that. Pfwoar, this was huge! She listened as Piet let the others on the airfield know what had happened. There was a lot of fuss and commotion, but Lena was now quite calm! What would her parents say?

She slowly undid the harness and stretched her fingers. They had actually got a bit cramped in the last hour. Lena grinned happily.

All at once she saw something coming her way from her right. It was a good half a football team running towards her. Ahead of the pack, that was – of course, Philipp. The game. She had almost forgotten.

Lena opened the canopy. All of a sudden she went weak at the knees and couldn't get out. Her hands trembled a little. Then, there he was, standing in front of her.

'Couldn't wait till Monday?' asked Philipp with a grin.

Lena laughed heartily. She pulled herself up, slipped out of the parachute, stretched her legs and climbed out of the glider. Luckily, now that she had solid ground under her feet the trembling stopped. She was now standing right up close to him. She prodded his chest gently.

'Nope, and you?'

He kissed her tenderly – cautiously even, as if she might take off again and disappear at the first sudden movement. When he saw that she was still there, standing in front of him with wide eyes and rosy cheeks, looking at him and laughing, he took her in his arms and held her tightly.

Philipp gave a wide smile.

'Not a second longer! But flights from here to Moorbach are so hard to come by!' Another kiss. They both grinned self-consciously as the other footballers huddled around them excitedly. Lena fluttered her eyelids at him playfully.

'Really? I hadn't noticed! *I CAN FLY!*'

Glossary

Aerobatics Manoeuvres

Loop
A full circle flown vertically
Roll
A rotation around the longitudinal axis
Stall Turn
The aircraft flies up vertically then rotates on its yaw axis and flies vertically down again, also called a Hammerhead
Spin
Not only in aerobatics, but also in training for emergencies, yawing flight in a partly stalled condition, the aircraft spirals downwards

Aerotow

Launching method, the glider is towed up to release height behind a powered aircraft using a long rope

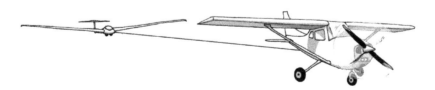

Aircraft parts

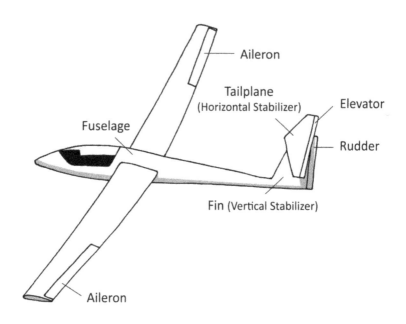

Ailerons
Control the aircraft in roll (bank left/ bank right)
Elevator
Controls the aircraft in pitch (nose up/ nose down)
Fuselage
The body of an aircraft to which the wings, undercarriage
tailplane etc are attached
Rudder
Controls the aircraft in yaw (nose left/ nose right)

Alphabet

In aviation, individual letters are given code words, so they can easily be understood on the radio. They're used often, for example in aircraft call signs. They are: **A**lpha, **B**ravo, **C**harlie, **D**elta, **E**cho, **F**oxtrot, **G**olf, **H**otel, **I**ndia, **J**uliet, **K**ilo, **L**ima, **M**ike, **N**ovember, **O**scar, **P**apa, **Q**uebec, **R**omeo, **S**ierra, **T**ango, **U**niform, **V**ictor, **W**hiskey, **X**-ray, **Y**ankee, **Z**ulu

Briefing

Meeting of the pilots/crew before a flight
(Debriefing – after the flight)

Call Sign/ Registration

Aircraft markings to identify individual planes. Also used on the radio with the ICAO alphabet. Usually a one or two letter country code followed by a three or four letter individual call sign for the aircraft, eg G-EAOU (= Golf-Echo Alpha Oscar Uniform). In some countries, glider call signs use a different system to powered planes

Centre of Gravity

The balance point of a body, in this case an aircraft including the crew. If the aircraft were suspended from this point it would not tip in any direction. If the cockpit is too heavily loaded, the centre of gravity will be too far forward. This makes it difficult to circle and land correctly. If the cockpit is too lightly loaded, the centre of gravity will be too far back. This makes it harder (or impossible) to recover from a spin.

Spinning, and most importantly recovering from a spin, can be practiced at height to learn how to cope in an emergency, but it is essential not to enter a spin at low altitudes. It is important to always take care with cockpit loading

Cessna

There are many models of powered aircraft made by Cessna Textron Aviation. In this book a C182 is used as a glider tow plane

Circuit

After take-off a 90° turn to the left (or right for a right hand circuit) is made onto the crosswind leg, then another 90° left to the opposite heading as the runway for the downwind leg, then comes the base leg, and finally the final approach, flown along an imaginary extension of the intended landing path

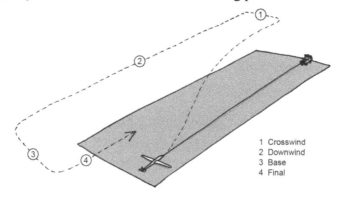

1 Crosswind
2 Downwind
3 Base
4 Final

Cloud Base

Altitude of the lowest part of a cloud

Cross Country Flights

If the thermals are good enough, glider pilots usually want to fly somewhere. Typical flights are often out and return (a flight to a distant point and back home), or triangles (to a distant point, then a third point, and then home again).

The achieved distance is the distance around the relevant points. There are also races.

A 50km flight is a required part of training in most countries. Further distances, 300 km, 500 km etc., can be officially recorded and badges awarded to recognize the achievement

Cumulus

The puffy white clouds often seen in a blue summer sky, cumulus clouds mark thermals, the cloud is formed when the thermal pushes moist air to a height where it gets cold enough for the moisture to condense

Dolly

Fitting to attach to a glider, often with one or more wheels mounted on it to help move the glider around on the ground or mount it in the trailer. Can be a fuse dolly (under the belly), tail dolly, wing dolly, etc.

Gliders

ASK21
Two-seater glider made from composite material, capable of aerobatics and often used in training (in this book also called 21 for short)

ASK23
Composite single seater, often used in training because of its similarity to the ASK21

ASW19, LS4
Composite single seater aircraft for advanced pilots

K8
Older single seater of mixed construction (wood, steel tube, fabric), often used early in training

ICAO

International Civil Aviation Organisation, determines international aviation standards, for example Language, standard phraseology, Alphabet, aviation-maps etc.

Kavalierstart

Pulling the glider into a steep climb too early in a winch launch. This is dangerous because if the cable breaks, there may not be enough height to recover into a normal flight attitude before hitting the ground. The name kavalierstart comes from German and is related to both having a cavalier attitude to safety and the way a cavalry horse can rear up at a similar angle to a glider on a winch cable

Knots

Wind speed and air speed are measured in knots in many countries. Knots are nautical miles per hour. 1 knot = 1.85 km/h = 1.15 mph

Launch Emergency Training

It's always possible that the launch cable or aerotow rope could break during the launch.

The glider pilot has to know what the options are for every phase of the launch if the rope or cable breaks.

Is there still enough room to land straight ahead? Is there enough height to turn around 180 degrees and land with the wind on the runway (downwind landing)? Or, is there even enough height to fly a modified circuit and land into wind on the runway?

Leading Edge

The front part of a wing or other flying surface which the air strikes first in flight. Collects insects that need to be washed off at the end of the day

Lepo/ Launch point bus

Vehicles for transporting all the necessary equipment to the launch point and to retrieve the winch cables. Lepo is a term used in Germany based on the car brand Opel. It is an abbreviation for Leporello (oller Opel backwards). *Oller Opel* just means old Opel

Licence

All countries with gliding operations have relevant authorities or organisations that regulate gliding. Training is very similar everywhere, but in some countries no licences are issued. Check with the relevant people in your country to find out details like how old you need to be to start learning. It's usually easy to find this information online. In Germany, you need to be 14

Logger

GPS (Global Positioning System) based electronic device for recording where a glider flies. Provides evidence and information about cross-country flights, especially in competitions. Logger files can be used as evidence for badge and record flights and to upload online for comparison with other pilots and other clubs.

Some countries have regional and nationwide competitions accessed by uploading logger files

Slipping/Skidding

It's best to fly a glider so that the airflow comes from directly ahead. This gives the least drag which means you can glide further. If the pilot doesn't fly accurately, the airflow isn't from directly ahead, but strikes the fuselage slightly to one side. This produces more drag and the aircraft sinks faster. In a turn, the aircraft nose lags behind the turn when slipping and gets ahead of the turn when skidding.

Stick

The main control column in many aircraft. In gliders, the pilot holds the stick in the right hand. Forward/aft movement controls pitch. Left/right movement controls roll

Spin Training

See "Aerobatics Manoeuvres" and "Centre of Gravity"

Thermals

Rising air masses. The sun heats the ground and the ground heats the air in contact with it. A layer of air is produced at ground level that is warmer and lighter than the air above it. Eventually it will rise in a stream. The stream of rising air is the thermal. Around the thermal, air moves down to replace the rising air.

When flying into this falling air on the way to the thermal, the glider first sinks, then rises when entering the thermal. On the way out of the thermal, it sinks again.

This can feel like the glider is falling out of the sky, but there are no such things as air pockets! Glider pilots seek out thermals to gain height by circling in the rising air mass and being carried up with it. The height gained can be used to glide to the next thermal and so on to fly cross-country.

Sink	Lift
An area of falling air	An area of rising air

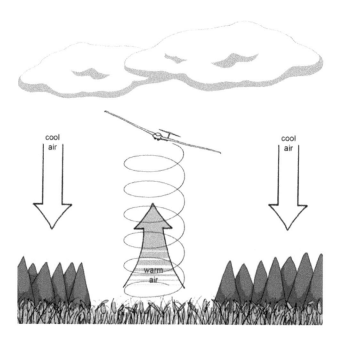

Trim

Adjusted by the pilot to reduce stick forces in flight so that holding a particular nose attitude needs less effort

Undercarriage

The wheels of an aircraft. Usually all the wheels of one aircraft together are collectively referred to as "The Undercarriage"

Vario

Variometer – shows the rate of climb or descent of a glider. Audio-varios are electronic instruments that give the information in the form of an audible tone (beeps high tones for climb and low tones for sink)

Winch Launch

A winch pulls in a very long cable very fast with the help of an engine. The glider is hooked onto the end of the cable and the winch gives it flying speed. The glider pilot can steer the glider into a steep climb, like how a kite flies. Significantly cheaper than aerotow

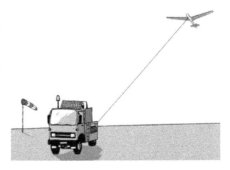

More about Lena:

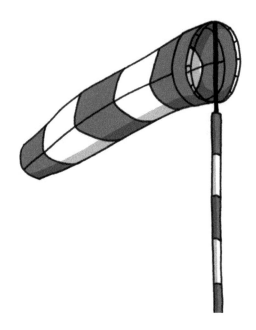

www.lena-book.com

The Author: Judith E. Spörl

was flying gliders before she even had her driving licence.

She has enjoyed cross-country gliding in Australia and loves aerobatics. Now she works as an air traffic controller in Salzburg, Austria.

Judith wanted to share her enthusiasm for aviation with her young daughter who just wasn't interested, so she decided to share her experiences in fictional stories. *Lena fliegt sich frei* and *Lena startet durch* became great successes in Germany and her daughter really got fired up.

The Illustrator: Doreen Goedhart

actually has a terrible fear of flying and has only flown once – on the other hand she can now draw an ASK21 in her sleep! She is a qualified graphic designer and illustrator and has had her own studio since 2011.

More about Doreen:

www.doreens-art.de

The Translator: Brendan English

has been working in Solar Electronics for over 25 years. Since he was a small boy he always knew he wanted to fly but wasted many years and didn't take up gliding till age 34.

Brendan learns German as a hobby and has translated many articles for gliding magazines and websites. Piet, the gliding instructor, is his favourite character in *Lena Earns Her Wings*. Perhaps that's because Brendan is also a gliding instructor? He and his wife Jana live in Australia where they fly long flights together in their two-seat glider every summer.

CPSIA information can be obtained
at www.ICGtesting.com
Printed in the USA
LVHW02s2213270818
588257LV00006B/76/P